Holidays

in August Grove

The

August Grove Collection

Coming soon from
The August Grove Collection

HOLE Cards
Book 1 of The Coffin Chronicles

When Dash Coffin returns to August Grove to help find missing children, she finds she's not the hunter but the prey in a game with a killer so powerful even her magical poker deck is helpless against him.

FOG3 Case 1: Even Bones Lie
Book 1 of The FOG3 Investigation Files

From the FOG3 Investigations' case files comes their first August Grove case. A young woman who disappeared twenty years ago is now back visiting her fiancé. The man hires Frank Gamble and the FOG3 team to find her long missing bones.

The

August Grove Collection

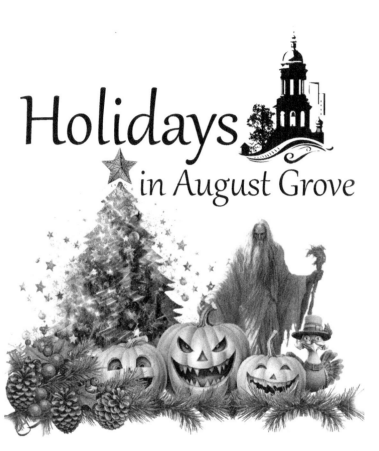

Holidays
in August Grove

Holiday Tales from the August Grove Herald

as told to

Sybil Ward

Crystal Orb Publishing
1550 15th St.   Augusta, GA USA
https://crystalorbpublishing.com

ISBN 979-8-9894399-1-1
Holidays in August Grove paperback edition October 2023
10 9 8 7 6 5 4 3 2 1

PEOPLE ARE TALKING

HOLE CARDS

"An engaging opener that's fun, fast-paced, and full of heart. You're going to want to see more of Dash."

> J.D. Horn, USA Today Bestselling Author of
> The Witching Savannah Series

"The Painted Trunk is a fun, genre-bending romp. It's got an engaging heroine and a great premise, with enough twists and turns to keep the reader racing headlong through its pages."

> Barbara Rogan
> author of A DANGEROUS FICTION

THANKS!

Thank you so much for purchasing

Holidays in August Grove

Get free stories and read more about the shenanigans in August Grove. Download a free copy of the

Story Storm Newsletter.

SCAN THE CODE BELOW

This book is dedicated to lovers
of the holidays.
A Happy, Glorious, Merry, & Blessed
to you all!

Behold, the Holidays in August Grove

Come! Take my hand and grip it tight,
even holidays have a night!

Into the mirror you should look
And glimpse a very different book
See yourself within its pages
And all the holidays of the ages

Journey to our little town
Cloaked in Halloween's lovely gown
With pumpkins, spice and all things nice
The ghosts come calling in the night

Yuletide drinks, shout hurray
Let us party all this day
But what is this, a monster's frown?
Murder, mayhem hits the town

August Grove its twisted fate
In the Herald's stories shake
Thanksgiving shows its wondrous head
Christmas? You'd better stay in bed!

So, kick off your shoes, turn down the light
and read the whispers of a different night.

J .A. Cauldwell
The Scribe of Erinna

It's always a holiday… somewhere.

Throughout the world, humans seek opportunities to celebrate, because celebrations are reasons to be happy. Even our sadder gatherings will take on a brighter hue around the edges if attended by family or friends we haven't seen for many years. Alas, when we're all bogged down with the drudgery of life, it is sad to say, but true, that often the only time we see those we care about is at funerals.

The people in August Grove, Georgia are no different. They try to be together when they can, but even in a town this size, the chore of living often keeps them away from family and friends. Ah, but when they gather, it's always… eventful.

But before I continue, in case we haven't met before, I should introduce myself.

I am the August Grove Herald.

And unlike the town's rag of a newspaper, I am a true seer, and I've been one for hundreds of years. It is my blessing, my curse, and my purpose to relay what is occurring and what is yet to arrive. But I can never interfere.

As a herald, I am compelled to tell someone what I know. That is my purpose. But I never, ever inform those whom my knowledge would benefit most. To do so would bring destruction upon me, and to all whom I have confided.

Thus, is my life.
That is my curse.
But you…
I will tell you everything. It is you who will bear witness.

I am the Herald.

Hear me.

On this occasion, I come with stories of the holidays. Some stories are told by others, but I relay them to you so that you might get a taste of what August Grove is like during its cheerier times. Even during feasts and celebrations, the unusual, strange, and bizarre slip into the corners and taint the edges. Sometimes for good, as you will see.

And just for fun, I thought I'd show you some of my exines, or outer selves, as we go through the holidays. In my time in this world, I've been almost every race, a multitude of ethnicities, and both sexes. My rebirth means a change to my outer form, and my abilities might get a tweak, but where it's important, I'm the same… person. Sometimes there's a slight change to my personality, but that's due primarily to societal changes. But one thing is constant: I am August Grove's Herald.

So, let the celebrating begin. Here I present some of the more entertaining moments in our little town. I give you…

Holidays
in August Grove

OCTOBER

In THE UNITED STATES, we have a few well-recognized holidays in the spring, a couple during the summer, but by far, the festivals that occur after the harvest, in the fall, are the largest on August Grove calendars. For that reason, I start our tour in October with my favorite holiday of the year, Halloween.

Tonight, we drop in on some of our friends at the town's main public library. The August Grove Pumpkin Party has been a tradition since the 1800s. Adults bring their little ones, dressed as jack-o'-lanterns, for a few hours of games, snacks, and, of course, scary stories. It's all good fun, even for the grown folk, with the library and its keepers adorned in the best holiday fashion.

There are three areas set up for storytelling. The little ones get their stories in the middle of the first floor, with lots of fluffy pillows and blankets, snacks, and enough light that it's not really frightening. Three of the librarians, in their pastel witchy costumes, team up to act out some of the kids' favorite stories.

Teens and easily frightened adults get the darker corner in the back, with flashlights and plenty of hot chocolate. Kids from the two high schools select this storyteller via vote. The winner is usually a teacher, and it's always someone capable of spinning a great yarn. Original stories only, and the more dramatic portrayals get the loudest applause and the most return visits.

Upstairs, in total darkness with candles, are the adults who are still young at heart or just lovers of a good story. The storyteller here is usually the main librarian, but unfortunately, tonight the wonderful Abigail Cline has come down with an awful cold, leaving the adults stranded without a tale.

Until someone volunteers.

Meet Randall James Canaday—Randy to almost everyone in town, and Sergeant First Class Canaday of the August Grove Police Department. Randy always volunteers to act as security at the library on Halloween, primarily so he can listen to the stories. But tonight, with the last-minute cancellation, Randy takes on a new role.

Tonight, Sergeant Canady is a storyteller, and he has a new spin on an old tale.

Trick or Treat - A Halloween Carol

IN THE DARK CORNER beside the refrigerator, Randy stared into the eyes of his beautiful wife, Ardis. They were upstairs in the crafts room of the main August Grove Public Library, and Randy thought he'd never seen her look so scared. "You don't think I can do this?"

She shrugged. "I love you, sweetheart, and I believe you can do anything you set your heart on doing…"

"But?" he asked.

"You're funny when you want to be." Ardis took his hands. "How often do you tell stories? Do you do that at the station? Because I don't think I've ever heard you…"

Randy gave her hands what he hoped was a reassuring squeeze. "No, I don't. I mean, I haven't. But when I was a kid, I watched all the creepy shows and movies. And remember those comics you made me get rid of?"

"The ones with that skinny demon thing?" she shivered. "I hated those books."

He laughed. "Yeah, you did." He pulled her into a hug. "I won't embarrass you. I promise." He pushed her away and smiled before tapping his head. "I've got some good stories in there."

His wife smiled. "OK, Master Canaday. Go out there and knock 'em… well, not dead. You know what I mean."

They hugged again, and Ardis left him to prepare. Randy didn't have a costume, and his uniform didn't exactly scream "skilled storyteller," but he sucked in a deep breath, adjusted his pistol belt, and strode out to his audience.

The double-wide table, actually four tables slid together, stood in the center of the library's craft room. People, three rows deep, surrounded the makeshift platform, and they all clapped as he approached.

"Thanks," Randy said. "I know Mrs. Cline usually sits cross-legged in the middle of the tables, but that's not happening tonight."

Everyone laughed.

"But if we can pull the tables apart, I'll drag a chair in, so I'll still be in the center of the story."

They all agreed, nodding and standing to pull their chairs back. As the group rearranged the furniture, Randy went off to find an office chair.

Everything was ready when he returned, and he pulled the office chair, with its swiveling base, into the new hole at the center of the tables. He removed his hat and placed it on a table as his audience lit their candles.

"Ready?" he asked.

A chorus of "Yes" came back.

"Alright, Ardis. Turn off the lights."

Randy lowered his head, and for almost a minute, he stayed that way, unspeaking. Just as the group began to mutter, he raised his head and said in a voice no one recognized…

"Welcome to the August Grove township. It is October 31, 1930, and the weather has assumed a decidedly pre-winter chill. In fact, the town has seen the coldest temperatures on record for two consecutive mornings, bringing much concern for the area's cotton crop. As the day bears on, the temperature rises, but there is still a deep cold riding the breeze, and clouds darkening the horizon. The wind is whispering in the narrow places, and candles and lamps are being lit against the dark."

"But despite the cold and gloom of the evening, a few of August Grove's hardiest and fun-loving children are taking to the streets in search of treats and scary good times. And pranks. Always jokes and pranks."

All while he spoke, Randy spun slowly, catching everyone in his gaze, his lowered voice making a few of them grin nervously.

"This is the night—Halloween, with fun and treats for all. But there's at least one person who is not in the mood for any of it."

THE FULL MOON PLAYED HIDE-AND-SEEK behind the billowing black clouds rushing across the night sky. Its pale beams lent a drizzle of light to the dozing lawn as the moon rose above the yard's shivering oak. As Emily Breakfield slammed closed the shutters and extinguished the porch lantern, the whispering wind tugged at her skirts and tossed leaves from the yard about her feet. This was the type of night she expected. Hooligans all. Even the wind. She stepped inside and shut the door firmly behind her.

"That'll be enough of that."

She was in August Grove to visit her uncle, Luther Bradford Killgore, the owner and publisher of the August Grove Herald newspaper. August Grove Herald. She allowed the name to rest on the tip of her mind for a moment. Her uncle had some kind of inspiration… or stroke… last year and changed the paper's name from the August Grove Tribune. She found neither name more inspirational than the other, but Uncle Luther had been odd of late. He'd taken to feuding with an old black woman over the oddest things, including the name of his newspaper, and the ownership of his house.

So bizarre.

Tonight, he insisted the house stay alight all evening for any children who might come seeking candy. "Trick or treating" is what he'd called it. She'd never heard the like. And with that, he had retired for the night, leaving her with the duty of doling out treats.

"Utter foolishness. In my opinion, the law should punish any parent who allows their child out tonight." Emily crossed her arms, mimicking her mother's favorite stance. She had no children of her own, but she was certain all—adults and their little ones—ought to be home in a warm bed on a night like this, just as she was going to be. She had extinguished all the lights because she had no intention of entertaining rapscallions all evening. "Halloween and… what is it again? Trick or Treat?" She snorted. "Absolute rubbish."

She crossed to the desk in the alcove beyond the foyer. She picked up her uncle's photograph and considered his face. In the years of her childhood, she had found her uncle dashing with his firm jaw and deep-set eyes. But he had changed so much. Most of his altered appearance had to do with age, of course, but the odd and furtive ways his eyes moved, the sour set of his mouth… she felt certain there was some sort of emotional malady he was coping with, and the family had sent her to… well, to keep watch over him.

"Such a shame." She replaced the photograph and reached for a book from the shelf above. The Seven Dials Mystery by Agatha Christie. She dearly loved a good mystery, and she'd been wanting to read this novel. With a smile, she pulled the book down, but her smile waned as she glanced at the door. Perhaps it wouldn't hurt to check the locks one more time.

"Look at yourself, Emily Louise Baily. Uncle's oddness is beginning to affect you."

She clutched the novel to her chest and shivered.

Luther had told the entire family about the ghosts who supposedly changed his life. Her mother had laughed and told him we had all read Mr. Dicken's Christmas Carol. But he shook his head adamantly. "This is no Christmas story," he said. "And who would want you to believe such an occurrence happened at Christmas? There might have been a shred of credibility to that story if Scrooge's encounter with the sheeted dead had happened on Halloween."

Her uncle had slapped his palms on the dining room table, startling even the maid. "No. She did it. That so-called herald. She sent those things… ghosts… to tell me of the wrongdoings of our grandfather, and to warn me I was on the path toward much the same. They were civil war soldiers and—"

"Brad!" Mother was the only person on earth who could call her brother by his childhood name. "Please control yourself. No one is questioning your veracity, but you must admit, ghosts… in your…" Mother raised an eyebrow. "Where did this… event… occur?"

He sat back and straightened his tie, but the harsh, haunted look in his eyes remained. "The event, as you call it, happened in my home, of course. This past October, on Halloween. All Hallows Eve, as some refer to it, the—"

"Luther," father said, "is this some sort of joke?"

"Sam, you've known me over thirty years," my uncle said. "Have you ever known me to joke?"

Daddy frowned. "No. No, I can't say I have. Not even at university."

"I'm not a joking man. That woman… that witch… she sent them because I changed the name of the paper to Herald. I had found a note in father's papers, one written by Grandpa Earnest. Grandpa had intended to change the name of the paper, but he died that very night. So, to honor him…"

"That's a wonderful reason to change the name," mother said. "What is this woman's objection?"

Perspiration beaded on my uncle's face, and he wiped it away with his dinner napkin. "She says she is the only herald in August Grove, and as long as the paper bears that name, I can expect to have… trouble. Troubles. That's what she said. And I have. From broken gears in the press, to my employees coming down with strange maladies, to—"

"But those are just normal inconveniences," father said.

Luther cast his eyes around the table as if searching for help. "Yes, and I treated them as such. That's why she sent the ghosts."

"That's quite enough," mother said. "We… we believe you, Luther. All right? Let's just finish dinner before we discuss this further."

But they didn't.

That was three years ago.

There were plenty of stories her uncle might have told that night. "But ghosts?" She loved the old man, but balderdash. All of it. Yet he persisted with the tale every time one of them asked.

She took her dripping candle from the desk and, as she passed, grabbed her shawl from the nearby settee. Uncle Luther was every bit as stubborn and cheap as that character, Scrooge. To her mind, he could do with a dose of generosity, wherever it came from. Emily drew the shawl around her shoulders and shivered as she muttered, "This house is like a tomb."

But two bowls of fresh apples and treats sat on the console table beside the door. Real candies! She couldn't imagine what he paid for those. "He should have spent that money on coal."

The pendants on the table's astral lamp tinkled at the rapping on the door. Emily snorted and moved off toward the sitting room, where she had a warm fire by which to read her book.

However, the rapping persisted. Unable to settle into her novel with all the noise, she returned to the door. "Go away!" she shouted through the wooden panels.

"Trick or treat!" came the cheerful replies.

Emily cracked the door. Three tiny children, less than waist high and draped in white sheets, stood with their pillowcases held high.

"We have nothing for you. Go away!" She started to close the door.

"Mr. Killgore always has treats for us," one of them said.

"It's a bargain he made with our brothers," said the second.

"If you don't give us our treat, our brothers will come next with a trick," said the third.

"Balderdash and malarky! Get off my porch." Emily slammed the door.

By 10pm, Emily was deep in her book. No children had called after the ghosts, and she'd enjoyed the evening. Only embers glowed in the grate when, again, there came a sharp rapping at the door. "Why aren't the little monsters in bed?"

She flung open the door to find three full-sized ghosts, white sheets drifting, with baleful red eyes peering at her. "Trick or treat," they said.

She glared at them. "You three are too old to be out begging. Begone."

"We came for our bargain," one ghost said.

"You treat or we trick," said the second.

Said the third in a grumbling tone, "Treats and good fun or our fathers will come."

"And they'll face my gun!" Emily slammed the door. "Face my gun." She laughed all the way up to her bedroom.

The chiming of the old clock woke her at midnight. That clock hadn't worked since she was a child. She sat up in bed, a shiver scurrying down her spine. Sounds… No, words… booming like claps of thunder.

"Trick or Treat!"

Three creatures of horrible countenance, perhaps ghosts since they were translucent, hovered at the foot of her bed, accompanied by the near-deafening clank of chains and howling wind. Curtains swung out and away from windows, and the bed's heavy drapes billowed and flew. Emily cowered beneath her quilts, too terrified to move or scream. Where was her uncle?

"The bargain was broken," said the shortest.

"You provided no treat," said the one in the middle, his head speaking from beneath his arm.

"'Tis the trick, then," boomed the tallest.

EMILY AWOKE TO THE SOUND of her uncle calling her name. Squinting, confused by the bright sunlight streaming into her eyes, she blinked several times, trying to orient herself to the view… of the garden… because it was upside down.

Upside down.

She first tried to speak, then to scream. Emily could do neither. The slippery hull… the sweet taste when her teeth punctured it… an apple? There's an apple in my mouth?

"Emily, please nod if you're able," her uncle said.

She tried to oblige… obey… but she couldn't. A picture formed in her terrified mind, an image of her hanging, trussed up like a suckling pig with a ruby red apple forced into her mouth. "Uncle" was unintelligible from her stuffed mouth, and tears flowed back across her forehead and off the side of her face. The words she wanted to say, the plea for help, lay strangled in the back of her throat.

In due course, though it seemed a lifetime, someone arrived with a ladder, and the men gently untied her and lowered her onto a blanket at her uncle's feet. There was concern etched deep in his face, but there was also tittering from the people who had gathered beyond the gate. She would have loved to have told them off, but all she could do in the moment was cry as her uncle worked to remove the apple jammed between her teeth.

"Please, dear, just be still," her uncle said. But she noted the quirk of his lips. He wanted to laugh as well.

It wasn't until she was free of the twine or whatever bound her that her senses acknowledged the other… the other…

She screamed.

If the neighbors didn't know something was awry, they knew after that. Emily imagined the sound might have shattered glass. But the sound wasn't such a noise because the night's cold air had parched her throat. The scream reverberated inside her head so loudly because her ears were plugged. Stuffed. With candy.

As she sat up, she realized the only… opening… of her body that wasn't… stoppered, were her eyes. She felt it. Everywhere. Even within her brassiere. The tittering became full-blown laughter as she began snatching gumballs, caramel cubes, and candy buttons from her ears.

Humiliating was not a strong enough word!

"Take her inside," her uncle yelled. "Now!"

Two of the men helped her to her feed, and then a third hoisted her into his arms. He carried her up the steps and into the house as the laughter escalated to a roar. Her uncle shouted before he closed the door behind them, "Get away! The show is over!"

Show? Is that what he called this? Emily pulled yet more candy from her ears.

"Sir, what should I... do with her?" the man carrying her asked.

"Put me down!" Emily shouted through a wall of tears. "Put me down and get out!"

The men did as she demanded. As soon as the door closed, she fell into her uncle's arms, weeping as she had never wept in her life. None of this had damaged her physically, but the humiliation cut as no knife could. "How, Uncle... how could this happen?" She twitched as something scratched her from inside her underwear. Emily wanted to scream again. "This is impossible!"

"Now, now, Emmy. Come along upstairs and we'll..." He stared at her bosom. "I mean, I'll get the maid to come up and help you with... that."

She supposed he held it as long as he could, but that didn't make it any less painful when he smiled. "They... they tricked you... quite hard, I'm afraid."

"Tricked me. Tricked me?" Emily suddenly coughed, and two chunks of chocolate exploded from her mouth. She stared down at the floor where the candy lay before tears rained anew.

"There, there, my girl." Her uncle guided her over to the settee. "Uh, can you... can you sit?"

"No," she whispered.

In the next breath, she sneezed, and candy buttons poured from her nose.

This was apparently the key to her uncle's gate. He stared at her for a second before he threw his head back and howled. He laughed for what Emily considered an unseemly long time. "Are you finished?" she finally asked through sniffles.

He wiped his eyes and nodded before calling for the maid.

The woman arrived, apparently expecting an injury. She carried towels and bandages, but halted when she noted the candy-strewn floor at Emily's feet. Emily burst into new tears, causing more candy buttons to leak from her nose.

"Please escort my niece upstairs and… assist her."

As his charwoman made to take Emily's arm, her uncle patted her shoulder. "My dear, this was a harsh lesson, but one well learned, I think. Never enter the space between debtor and collector, especially when you have scorn for the bargain. That brews an animosity which makes retribution so much harsher. Remember Emily, no matter what you believe, you must take a person at their word until you have proof otherwise, because the space between debtor and collector is often fraught with fright."

Emily nodded as the maid led her away up the stairs. She would never speak of this to anyone. And she would return home immediately. If questioned by her parents, she would report that her uncle was in fine form, aware of his responsibilities, and attending to all of his debts.

R ANDY SLOWED, STOPPED, and lowered his chin to his chest. He waited.

A clap.

And then another.

Followed by chairs sliding back and people rising to give him a standing ovation.

The police officer raised his head, smiling, and sought the face of his wife. He found her, waving her candle, and grinning broadly at the back of the room.

"A star is born," someone said.

Randy's grin broadened. Maybe so.

Ardis waited for him near the front entrance while everyone shook his hand and told him how much they loved the story, and the librarians each begged him to consider returning next year as a storyteller. Randy smiled and promised to consider another performance, even as he was already searching his interior database for another story that was bigger and better—

"So, is that hat going to fit on your head now?" Ardis asked, her grin perhaps larger than his own.

"Let's see." He donned his cap and winked at her. "Just barely."

They laughed, linked arms, and followed the last of the crowd out of the library. "Randy, where did you get that story? It was so funny."

"That one…" he said as he pulled her closer and put his arm around her shoulders, "I collected the night I got Miss Miranda drunk."

Ardis stopped and gaped at him. "You did what?"

He laughed and tugged her back into step with him as they continued down the walk. "Remember the accident Faith had a few years ago? Well, Miss Miranda was crying and saying, 'God, why can't I see?' So, I took her down to the bus station and got Mavis to make her one of her infamous milkshakes…"

NOVEMBER

WHAT IS THE PRICE OF COMPANIONSHIP?

Can you imagine being so lonely you'd be willing to do anything just to see a friendly face? Can you imagine being sick with want of someone to talk to?

There are thousands of people who long for companionship every day, and they're not always who you suppose. Yes, there are lonely seniors, sad disabled people, and isolated souls because of mental and emotional issues. But the bulk of the lonely are able-bodied and of sound mind, but something, or some condition, prevents them from connecting with others. Keeps them away from friends.

And the need to have company in your life only worsens with the holidays. The thought of celebrating with family and friends is a dull knife in a lonely person's heart.

So, if you were trapped in loneliness, forced to be alone, how far would you go to escape?

When Portia Tate finds herself without family, cut off from her friends, and surrounded by hostile neighbors, she realizes even the swank surroundings of a luxury hotel aren't enough to replace those you care about. Portia comes to know what true loneliness is, and learns to what extremes she's willing to go for a friendly conversation.

Only the Lonely

Chapter 1

THE MIDDAY SUN streamed from the living room straight to the front door, providing Portia Tate a moment of blindness, but also a second of how it felt to be in the spotlight. The day maid rushed across the room, apologizing as she pulled the window's lush draperies closed.

Once again able to see, Portia entered the apartment with a bellman at her heels. "You don't have to worry about that, Juanita. I had to shut those curtains from noon until two o'clock every day."

"Yes, ma'am," the young maid replied.

"And you don't have to ma'am me. I'm still Portia. Living here ain't going to change me."

The bellman cleared his throat.

"You expecting a tip, Oscar?"

"I am," the man said with a big grin. "You always tipped me well before, so if you haven't changed…" He winked at Juanita.

Portia laughed. "Well, I was tipping you then with Mr. Lowe's money. He left me the apartment, but there wasn't a check with that. In fact, what little equity this place had, I had to sell it back to the Management Team to catch up on the dues. I can't catch a break."

"But this is a break, Miss Portia," Juanita said, her big brown eyes wide. "You own it, so you can sell it to anyone you want.

There are a thousand people on the waiting list to move into the Belmonte. When we found out Mr. Lowe left it to you, we had a party. One of us, living upstairs. Living good."

Portia dropped her purse onto the coffee table and kicked off her heels. "I've always wanted to do that." She limped to the over-sized sofa and collapsed onto it.

"Unfortunately, I'm only here for a minute. I want to see what living among the high and mighty is really like, but I ain't got the cash to stay more than six months. I'll be able to have one of those fabulous Belmonte Thanksgivings, but after that, I want back in the rotation." She snorted.

"I asked for a leave of absence, you know, like professional people do when they have another project or want to stay home and sleep." She smiled. "I'll need to get my old job, the one before I got assigned to Mr. Lowe, but that might not happen. Betty Boo said…" Portia pushed her nose up with her finger and spoke with a nasal twang. "It won't be appropriate for you to return to your duties here after living among the residents. It will be better for everyone if you sell the apartment back to the board and forgo this, this…"

"This what?" Oscar asked.

"She didn't finish." Portia put her feet up on a pouf near the sofa. "I gave her that raised eyebrow, Mrs. Crane style. Puts Miss Betty right back in her place. I let her know I'm a resident for now, and she won't be talking to me like I'm a maid."

"I heard that." Oscar chuckled as he picked up Portia's bags again. "To the master bedroom, Madam?"

They all laughed, but then Portia shook her head. "No, take them to the guest room. I don't want to sleep in there."

Both Oscar and Juanita nodded their understanding.

"If I was going to stay here for good, I'd get rid of most of this stuff. I know these things are expensive, but they're drab and tired. I think Mr. Lowe left me this place because I always told him I hated it."

"No, you didn't!" Juanita perched on the piano bench.

"We laughed about it. Sometimes, he'd try to convince me to come on nights. He said the night maid wouldn't talk to him, and all the neighbors were fools, so he didn't want to talk to them. We'd hang out all day watching scary movies and playing cards and talking after I got my cleaning done."

She shrugged. "Sometimes I'd come in on a Sunday and cook for him. He was losing so much weight. Becky was alright company, he said, but her cooking was dangerous." She smiled. "I hated watching him waste away like that. When he left for the hospital, he told me he wouldn't be back, and the place would be all mine." Portia blotted a tear. "But I didn't believe him."

She gazed around the apartment. "He'd say, 'It's all glitz, Portia. People here aren't nice. I should've moved out years ago.'"

"Yeah, they're as snotty to each other as they are to us," Oscar said. "Remember when Mrs. Daly, down on four, died a few months ago? All they talked about was getting into her place to see what things she'd owned. The poor woman committed suicide, and they couldn't have cared less."

"I'd better run, Miss Portia," Juanita said. "Miss Betty will be looking for me."

"Yeah, me too," Oscar said.

"Wait." Portia grabbed her purse and rushed to the door. "Like always."

"No, this one's on us," Oscar said. "Welcome to the Belmonte, Miss Tate."

"Why, thank you, Oscar." Portia grinned. "I'll be down to see you guys later."

He stopped, his palm on the doorknob. "Not an option, Portia. House rules, remember? No fraternizing with the residents. You can't come down, and unless we have business, we can't come up."

Suddenly her purse weighed a ton, and Portia's arms dropped to her sides. "That doesn't apply to me."

Juanita stepped back into the door after glancing up and down the hallway. "Especially you. Miss Betty reminded us of the rules this morning, and she said no exceptions. We all figured she was talking about you."

"That cow! I'll…"

"You'll behave and have fun. We'll see you." Oscar patted her shoulder and moved into the hall after Juanita. "You've never worked nights here?"

"No," Portia said. "Place hopping at night?"

Oscar laughed. "Yeah, like a damned tomb. Nothing happening here after sundown but old boards, broads, and bones. That's it. But you keep this door locked."

"I don't get scared, Oscar," Portia said. "You know how I love my horror movies."

"This place ain't no movie." He reached in and turned the lock. "Keep this door closed and locked… especially after dark. Understand?"

Portia grinned. "Yes, daddy."

"Mock me all you want," Oscar said. "Just do as I say."

She placed her hand over his on the doorknob. "Wait. Is there something you're not telling me? I've never heard anything bad about the Belmonte."

"That's because you never worked at night." Juanita wrung her hands as she peered down the hall at the elevator. "We have to go, Oscar."

"I'm coming." He smiled at Portia. "Bye."

He departed, but Portia heard the doorknob rattle a few seconds later. She smiled. "That man worries too much."

Portia rushed off to the bedroom to unpack. She had only three hours to prepare for her first Belmonte ball as a resident. Enraptured, she often stood in the back hallway and peered through the kitchen peephole. The beautiful people twirled around the floor, and like Cinderella, Portia always dreamed of going to the ball.

Tonight, her dream would come true. She had spent a month's wages on her dress and shoes, and she had a lovely necklace Mr. Lowe gave her on her last birthday. It was a generous gift, and if she had known the state of his finances, she wouldn't have taken it. But she had, and now she'd wear it proudly.

AT 7PM, PORTIA OPENED HER DOOR, only to find a group of people gathered there. Before she could utter a word, a woman in a mint-green gown stepped forward and threw a scrunched piece of paper into her face. Portia's initial reaction was surprise rather than anger. She glanced down at the paper, which was a seating card, and saw her name on it. The match stood ready to light her fuse, but now a man spoke up.

"We know who you are, Portia Tate. Arthur Lowe has family he should have left his apartment to. How did you get into his will?"

Somewhere, a woman said, "Don't be so naive, Bruce. Sex. That's what her kind does. She was probably sleeping with him for years."

Portia's mouth opened, but her famous temper failed her. She couldn't find words for her rage. And her pain. She had done nothing to deserve this.

"Don't you dare come downstairs," the woman in the green dress said, "unless you're going back to work in the kitchen. How dare Betty put you at my table? I don't care what bed you sleep in, you're a damn maid, and you are not welcome in the dining suite or the ballroom."

Somehow, her arms moved. Somehow, her hand functioned, though Portia wasn't aware of it until the door slammed closed. Tears flowed until the pendant lying on her chest swam in them. Portia had barely spoken to another human being for a month. The other residents met her forays into the common areas with snarls and insults; or provided the cold view of a turned back. She couldn't visit her friends without getting them fired, and Betty accompanied them when they delivered a meal or responded to her call.

She was alone.

The thought of returning to her old apartment became more palatable, but she was alone there, too. Since her mother died and her sister moved away, Portia found herself all but isolated. She came to look forward to coming to work, to spending time with Mr. Lowe, and to seeing the rest of the staff. That had become her life, the staff, her family. Mr. Lowe's act of kindness, however, had taken her job from her.

Trips away from the Belmonte became fewer as even a trip to the market became a slow, twisting torture. Every store dripped with holiday decorations, from cartoon turkeys on the market's glass door, to the precocious baubles and Christmas decorations in the Dollar Saver. People seemed to stare at her, many with the same glares and snarls as her Belmonte neighbors. During her last trip to pick up a few groceries, the pointing and whispering became too much. She left her half-filled cart in the aisle and ran from the store. Portia hadn't been outside the building since.

Everything had gone wrong for her.

Including the apartment.

Now that she lived there, she understood Juanita's reluctance to be in the building after dark. The shadows came long and fast in the evening. And even with all the lamps on, those silhouettes seemed to defy the light, growing darker instead of fading away. There was a texture about them. The long, slithering shapes slid along the floor, running beside her as she moved from room to room, blacker than the darkness outside. Portia woke at least twice every night with the feeling those lightless blotches hugged the walls of her room, looming over her bed.

Even after she'd turned off the lights.

AUGUST GROVE WAS GROWING, embracing the new and polished century. Down the street from the Belmonte, with its old southern grace and charm, grew a new structure. The newest addition to Portia's tiny universe, Century Plaza, rose high above the tree line, stretching its steel arms toward the sky as if reaching for the sun. The tallest crane Portia had ever seen disappeared and then reappeared, over and over again, every day, lifting girders and supplies up to the helmet-wearing construction workers assembling that giant erector set. She had made of game of guessing how many times the crane would rise and fall in some number of hours. Watching that crane became the highlight of her day.

Portia had been in the apartment six weeks when there was a knock on the door one afternoon. She almost tripped while trying to reach the door before her visitor thought she wasn't home.

The smile awaiting her when she opened the door lifted her heart like the big crane down the block. Juanita was her usual nervous self, but she was smiling as if glad to see her. Without thinking, Portia pulled her into an embrace even as she dragged her across the threshold. "I'm so glad to see you."

Juanita detached herself from Portia, still smiling. "I'm happy to see you too, Miss Portia. I'm sorry about what's going on."

Portia tried to put on her old defiance. "It's alright. I've only got a few weeks left. I just miss being with all of you."

Juanita nodded. "I can't stay, but I brought you something. I got stuck with getting the last of Miss Daly's things out of her apartment. The family took what they wanted, but they're selling the apartment back to the Management Team, so I have to clean it. The good stuff is going to charity, but I saved this for you." She handed Portia the large plastic bag she carried. "I know you like scary movies and stuff, so, well… take a look.."

Portia took the parcel and walked over to the dining room. She laid the bag on the table before pulling out what was inside. "It's… it's a Ouija board. I… wow. I mean, I've never seen such a nice one."

The truth was, Portia had only seen Ouija boards in movies. But she had a reputation to maintain. "This must have cost. The family doesn't want it?"

Juanita shrugged. "Mr. John, her son, said the thing was too damned creepy. He told me to take it down to the furnace and throw it in."

Portia laughed. "You have to believe in the supernatural to think this board is scary. It'll be pretty on my table." She pushed the board into the center of the shining wooden surface. "Gorgeous."

Juanita nodded, but she was already moving to the door. "I've got to run. If Betty comes and I'm not there…"

"I understand. Thank you for the visit and the board."

As Juanita turned, Portia stopped her again. "Juanita… next Wednesday… will there be Thanksgiving dinner for the staff in the cafeteria?"

She grinned. "Yes, ma'am! Just like always. And this year there's an extra turkey, a gift from the Management Team. And we'll have the entire afternoon to celebrate. They're closing the kitchen to the residents so we can start Thanksgiving dinner early. Miss Betty said a lot of people were staying in for the holiday and inviting relatives and guests. Maids are getting double-time for helping in the kitchen. Real nice, right?"

Portia nodded as an icy knot formed in her stomach. "Yes."

It wasn't fair. They would all be there, like family. Cooking together, eating together, having fun. A real Thanksgiving in the Belmonte. Together. While she was stuck here, in this over-styled prison. It was so wrong. Portia clenched her teeth to keep back tears and harsh words. None of this was Juanita's fault.

"Yes, very nice."

The maid's smile broadened to a grin before she turned toward the elevator. Even as Juanita ran down the hall, shadows raced along the walls after her. Portia shoved the door closed and pressed herself against the wood. It wasn't even dark yet.

IT WAS TWO DAYS LATER when Portia, bored with solitaire and watching the crane, decided to play with the Ouija board. She didn't have a computer, but Mr. Lowe's cable subscription, which was good until the end of the year, had YouTube and a few other Internet programs with it. Information on the board game was easy to find, and she watched a few videos about how to use it.

Not what she'd call big fun, perhaps, but Portia thought the Ouija board could help her kill the afternoon.

Every person in the videos talked about having multiple players, a ghost you wanted to contact, and setting the ambience by dimming the lights, yada yada. Portia snorted. It was her board, so she'd play how she liked. She left the sun streaming in. As for the ghost...

Her heart pinched a little. She didn't want to think about her mother. That seemed disrespectful. Besides, she wasn't sure what she'd say to her. Tell her how much she missed her? Cry about her current woes? No, this was supposed to be fun, plus she loved her mother too much to disturb her.

But she hadn't known Mrs. Daly. Portia remembered her name, of course. Mrs. Daly had been a resident as long as Portia had worked in the hotel. But she couldn't remember what the woman looked like. Portia didn't think she had ever worked for her. "No disrespect if it's a stranger, right?" And since it had been her board, it might be easier to reach her.

"Listen to yourself, Portia Tate. Thinking about talking to ghosts." She wondered if that was any crazier than talking to herself.

At the dining table, Portia ran her fingers over the board. To her surprise, she got a mild shock. Probably because of whatever the board was made from—static electricity or something. She thought the board might be ivory, though Portia wasn't sure. The board was at least eighteen inches wide, as large as her breadboard, and twelve inches tall. It served as the lid to a wooden box underneath, attached with copper hinges. When she lifted the lid, she found the board's pointer, a triangle made from the same material as the board.

The lid, box, and pointer were all engraved. After studying the images on all sides for several minutes, Portia shivered. She conceded Mr. Daly had reason to call the box creepy. The beautiful images engraved in the edges of the board and the sides of the box were at the same time disturbing. Creatures of the underworld, demons and goblins and things she couldn't name, crouched and roamed across every inch. The board also contained the alphabet and words, carved and filled with what looked like ebony quartz or some other dark gemstone. It was the most intricate work Portia had ever seen.

And again, she shivered, as a shadow descended across the table as if someone stood behind her. She turned and peered back through the living room to the windows.

The midday sun streamed in, as usual, but it dimmed toward the center of the window as if something there filtered the light. As Portia watched, that shadow moved, sliding down the window to the floor. In the next instant, it slithered over the back of the sofa, over the seat, and down to the floor again. It was making its way toward her.

And the board.

The shadow slid over her, leaving a trail of goosebumps on her flesh. It glided across the table and seeped into the pointer. Portia gasped as the pointer, atop the board, spun clockwise three times. It stopped, aligned in the clear path between the letter groupings, pointing at nothing.

Portia rose from her seat, rubbing her arms. She didn't question her lack of fear. Even a spirit was better company than nothing. She bent and glared at the board. "That was some entrance. Is that you, Mr. Lowe?"

In the videos, the user had to put their hands on the pointer, so she sat down to receive the answer. Before she could touch it, however, the pointer slid, spun, and pointed to the word NO.

"Then who are you?"

The pointer spun, but stopped at NO.

No? What kind of answer is that? You won't tell me who you are?"

The pointer spun. NO.

"Well, then kiss my rump. I don't care." Portia turned away from the table. A banging sound caused her to look back. The pointer was rising and then falling back onto the board.

"What?" Portia went back to the table and took her seat. "What do you want?"

The pointer spun, but this time moved up to a letter. B.

Portia watched as the pointer darted back and forth, pointing to letters. L. O. O. D. It stopped.

"Blood? You want blood? What the hell?"

The pointer spun, this time twice, and then set out spelling again. P. A. Y.

"I have to pay you in blood? Seriously?"

In the center of the board, in the middle of the blank space between the letters, appeared another engraved image that had not been there before. It was a head, the face of a creature with enormous eyes and no nose. It also had a mouth that opened so wide, its eyes disappeared. The pointer set off spelling again.

P. A. Y.

"Oh, this is insane."

Yet Portia left the table to grab a steak knife from the kitchen. Scary, yes, but this was the most fun she'd had in months.

When she returned to the table, the pointer had moved back to center, pointing at the mouth.

Portia wasn't crazy about cutting herself, but she had nothing bloody to feed the thing. Not even hamburger. She clenched her jaw and poked the tip of the blade into her left middle finger. "Ouch!"

A drop of blood bubbled from the puncture. Portia peered into the mouth, but she saw no teeth or anything resembling a tongue. She held her finger over the dark hole and let two drops of blood fall in. She jumped back when the little demon's face rolled back into place. It smiled, the etched lines even cracking a little, before it faded away.

"Well?"

The shadow, darker now, slid out from the board, across the table, and draped across the dining room chair in its path. It... Portia could only think "thickened," but grew translucent as it resolved itself into a woman. The woman was like a faded image on a pane of glass. The spirit folded her hands in front of her on the table.

"Who... who are you?" Portia pressed her injured finger against her palm. The eyes of the spirit followed her movement.

"I said—"

"I understand. But I am... weak. It will... I cannot stay. I am... I am Jane."

Portia studied the ghost. She wore what might have been a house dress, blue with tiny flowers and a white collar. The woman must have been in her sixties when she died, though it was hard to be sure. Her lank blond hair had plenty of gray in it, and there were small wrinkles at the corners of her eyes and mouth. Portia wondered if dying made you look older, but she didn't want to waste her questions on things that didn't matter.

"Did you die here in the Belmonte?"

The ghost nodded.

"When?"

The woman frowned. "I... I don't remember. Perhaps... 1924."

"Wow. You've been away for a while."

The ghost did not respond, and Portia wasn't sure what else to say. After a minute, the ghost asked, "What do you want?"

"Want? I don't know." Portia grinned. "Are you a genie granting wishes?"

The ghost frowned but didn't otherwise respond.

"Sorry," Portia said. "Look, I just wanted somebody to talk to, you know? It's lonely here."

For the first time, the ghost seemed focused on her when she looked at Portia. "Lonely here."

Portia dropped onto her chair. "Yes, I knew you'd understand. People here are so mean. They won't talk to me, and I can't visit my friends, and everyone I love has left August Grove, so…" She stopped, surprised at how easily she revealed her pain to a person who wasn't alive. Portia regarded the fading figure. Maybe that was the point. She didn't have to worry about what she said to a ghost. "And I'm angry. The things they said to me…"

The woman nodded with her eyes fixed on Portia now. "Yes. I know…" Her voice became softer, as if she spoke from far away. "Must… go."

Portia leaned across the table. "No, please stay. I sublet my place for three months, so I can't go back home, so I can't get thrown out for visiting my friends, so I…"

The woman was like a wisp, and then nothing. The shadow eased back across the table and vanished into the board.

"No, come back." Tears rolled down Portia's face. "Please don't leave me alone."

The pointer spun, and when it stopped, the demon face had reappeared. It gazed up at her.

"So, you're hungry?"

The imp smiled, and the big mouth opened, causing the eyes to disappear.

"Fine." Portia poked and squeezed her finger until she reopened the wound, but only a bit of blood came out. She forced a single drop into the hole. And waited.

After a moment, the mouth closed, but the little demon didn't vanish. Instead, it frowned at her.

"What? You want more?"

The pointer spun, and then slid to the right to point at YES.

"Well, shit! We'd better have a good time for this."

The pointer spun twice before returning to point at the demon.

Portia grabbed the knife. She closed her eyes and poked the sharp tip into the hole in her finger, creating a larger cut.

"Damn!"

The demon's mouth opened as blood seeped from her wound. Portia hurried to let the flow drip into the hole. She let the demon feed while she counted to thirty.

Let the demon feed. That thought made her gut tighten. Portia snatched her hand back and clutched her finger. "That's enough."

The hole closed, and the demon smiled before vanishing. As before, the shadow slid out, away, and over to the chair. The woman materialized faster this time, and she was more visible. She regarded her hands before looking up at Portia. "Thank you."

Portia held onto her bleeding finger as she resumed her seat. "You need blood to stay… stay out here?"

"Yes." The ghost peered around. "A lot has changed since I left."

"I'll say. But you said the people haven't changed… or I thought that was what you were going to say."

She nodded. "Yes. They were mean and snobby when I lived here. My husband owned a hardware store, and he was a city councilman. He thought he was a bigshot. But we could barely make ends meet, him with his new suits and the crazy payments we had to make for this place. He took a loan from Tollie Albertson, that loan shark people say was kin to the police chief or somebody. Just to buy this apartment. Such a crazy thing to do. We had a nice little place on one of the tree streets… maybe Maple? I can't remember now." She paused for a moment, but then shook her head. "It doesn't matter. We were in a neighborhood with other people like us, but no…"

The story continued, with the ghost telling Portia how things were in the Belmonte back in the twenties. But far too soon for Portia, Jane faded. "I have to go now. And you should, too. It's dinnertime."

"It can't be that late." Portia gazed around. The apartment lay under deep shadows, and the thin yellow light from the streetlamps down on Greene Street dusted the windows. "We must have been talking for hours." She turned back to the woman, who had again returned to a shadow. "Wait. I can't go to the dining room, and I'm not hungry enough to order in. So we can talk some more, okay? Send your hungry pal back."

Portia jumped up and rushed into the kitchen. She returned with a white dish towel and a teacup. "I won't kill myself, but I can spare a little more blood."

The pointer spun four times, and the demon appeared while the ghost, returned to a wisp, hovered over the chair. Not giving herself a chance to wimp out, Portia grabbed the knife by its blade. It was razor keen, and it sliced her palm with hardly a sting. She held the cup and let blood flow into it. When the bottom of the cup was red and then some, she grabbed the towel and closed her fist around it.

"Okay, open up."

The demon smiled, and then the face gave way to the open mouth. Portia held the cup over the board and watched the blood disappear down the hole. "That's wild."

The demon's face didn't return that time. The hole vanished as the ghost reappeared. Again, Jane considered her hands, but then she looked up at Portia and smiled. "So, what do you want to talk about?"

Portia checked her hand. "I don't know. I enjoy listening to you."

The ghost leaned forward and smiled. "Why don't I tell you all about the people who live in the Belmonte… now?"

Chapter 3

PORTIA, THE TOWEL CLUTCHED IN HER FIST, gaped at the ghost across from her, now as vivid to her as any living being.

Jane sat back in her chair. "If you are interested, I can tell you many things about the people who live here. The walls—"

Portia laughed. "Wait. You mean the walls can talk?"

An almost normal-sounding chuckle came from the woman. Almost normal. The hairs on Portia's arms stood up.

"Yes, in a way. I think the walls and floors capture what we do in life. Like recordings. When you're… dead, you can see it. Hear it. Take Mrs. Abernathy…"

She had Portia's full attention. For the rest of the evening and far into the night, the ghost gave Portia the inside scoop on the Belmonte residents. She told her how Mrs. Abernathy, the woman in the green dress, had been having an affair with Oscar for years. And Bruce Gaters, the loudmouth in the hallway, was a prosecutor on the take from anybody willing to cough up a dollar. Before long, Portia was taking notes.

"What about Betty?" Portia asked.

"Oh, that one. She's got the best secret of all. That one sleeps with women—"

Portia shook her head. "No, Jane. That's not something we have to hide anymore. We don't judge—"

"I wasn't finished," Jane snapped. "She sleeps with the women in this building… For money."

"What? You mean…"

Jane grinned. "Yes. Betty is a prostitute to women. And she's got six regular customers in this building, and they're all married to men."

Portia fell back in her chair. "Well, well. Miss Everything By the Rules is a hooker on her days off."

"No." Jane laughed. "All the time. She doesn't have to take time off. She's in charge, so she checks on things throughout the day and…"

Her voice trailed off as she faded. "I must go."

Portia turned and gaped at the sun rising over the skyline. "We talked all night."

The ghost smiled as she disappeared. "Go down for breakfast."

Preoccupied with thoughts of revenge, Thanksgiving dinner, and time with her friends, Portia didn't say goodbye, as every video insisted, or notice whether the shadow returned to the board.

EARLY FALL MORNINGS IN AUGUST GROVE tended to be cool, but the sound of the furnace whirring on assured Portia that all was well in the Belmonte, and chilly hands and feet would not be an issue in the dining room as it was on some days. There would be nothing to ruin her breakfast—temperature or people.

With her hand bandaged, and dressed in a new teal ensemble, Portia waltzed into the dining room feeling like the world was hers to conquer. There were a dozen residents scattered about the room, and two of Portia's friends serving. Everyone gawked as she sat down at the center table.

A server rushed to her in apparent panic and blurted out under her breath, "What are you doing here?"

"Good morning, Becky." Portia's voice, even at normal volume, carried throughout the room. "I'd like scrambled eggs and ham, please, with a side of toast and orange juice. And if there's raisin toast, I'd like that instead of plain."

Becky leaned close to Portia and whispered. "There's going to be trouble."

Portia grinned. "I sure hope so."

On cue, Mrs. Abernathy left her husband and strode to Portia's table. "Didn't I tell you—"

"Were you raised in a barn, Mrs. Abernathy? It's customary to say good morning. Ah, but maybe that's why you sleep around like a whoring pig, because your mama raised you like one."

The woman stopped in mid-breath. She looked as if she might faint.

"If you're going to pass out, please take your ass back to your table first. I don't want you spoiling my breakfast."

Becky dropped her pad and pencil; across the room a glass crashed to the floor; and someone croaked, "Well, I never!"

Portia glanced around. "Yes, you probably did."

Mr. Abernathy was now at the table, supporting his wife, who was paler than Jane. "You can't speak to my wife like that, you—"

"Be careful what you say, Abernathy. I'm sure you don't want your wife to know what you do on your so-called poker nights."

"What's she talking about—"

He grabbed his wife's arm. "We're leaving." He stormed away, dragging his deflated wife with him, as the entire dining room erupted in buzzing chatter.

"Becky?"

"Yes, Portia?"

"Get my breakfast, sweetheart. And make sure I'm on the list for Thanksgiving dinner in the cafeteria… with my friends."

THE ATMOSPHERE IN THE DINING room still crackled with shock and curiosity half an hour later. Becky refilled Portia's glass and tumbler with juice and water, but she glanced around the room as she did, her eyes wide as if searching for a sniper or some other assassin. Portia smiled. "It's alright, Becky."

The young server leaned close. "Portia, it's going to be bad. They… the Abernathies… demanded Betty get in here and fix things… you."

Portia almost choked on her toast. "Oh, that's really good. Fix me."

Becky straightened. "You're… you're not worried?"

With the biggest smile she'd worn in a year, Portia said, "Just wait for it."

Portia was finishing her breakfast when a flushed Betty arrived. Her hair, pulled back from her narrow face, was damp, and she hadn't buttoned her suit jacket properly. The Belmonte's Chief of Staff glared at Portia with red-rimmed eyes as she snatched out a chair and sat down. "What are you doing?" she hissed.

Her chair squeaked as Portia pushed back from the table. She placed a ten-dollar bill beneath her plate before turning toward the kitchen.

Betty ran to cut her off. "Where are you going?"

"You're so full of questions, Betty." Portia, a good three inches taller, stepped closer and glared down into the woman's eyes. "Are you this inquisitive about your clients?"

Betty grabbed Portia's arm as she started once again toward the kitchen. "Where do you think you're going?"

"Any damned place I want," Portia said. "And if you like that hand, move it before something happens to it."

"I'll have you thrown out." Betty's sharp, rapid breathing was audible in the silence. No doubt, everyone in the room and beyond were listening. "You shouldn't be here, you uppity—"

"Please say it. Say it! I promise Mrs. Gaters will have to kiss a mouth with no teeth in it."

There was a collective gasp, a loud crash, and then people rushing around them. She and Betty, however, never broke eye contact.

"Who told you?" Betty growled.

"Told me?" Portia laughed. "Honey, I know every time you're down on your knees—"

Betty rushed forward until their noses almost touched. "Shut up. Just shut up." Fear had her eyes bouncing everywhere. "What do you want?"

"I want you off my case. I'll see my friends, and they're welcome to visit my apartment whenever they want. Got that? And you'll make that announcement during the morning and afternoon brief. And if you want me to stay away from the management group, put an envelope in my mailbox once a month until I leave here."

"Why you—" Her nostrils flared, but she mumbled between clenched teeth, "Anything else?"

"That will do. Now, excuse me. I want to say hello to everyone before I return upstairs."

THE KITCHEN STAFF GREETED PORTIA with applause, hugs, and handshakes. She even got a couple of kisses from men she had never met. It was a quick but joyous ten minutes. "I'd better let you all get back to work."

She scanned the room until she found Oscar. "Come here, you naughty man."

Oscar flushed beneath his brown skin. "You're well-informed, Portia, for someone who never worked nights."

"All you have to do is listen to the right people." She peered over his shoulder. "Where's Juanita? I wanted to thank her for my gift."

"She took off right after the brief this morning. I think she's got to have the Daly apartment ready for showing tomorrow."

Portia nodded. "I won't disturb her, but if she needs help with the packing and cleaning, I'd love to help her out. She gave me a major lift out of my misery. I owe her big."

Oscar raised an eyebrow but didn't ask questions. "I'll let her know."

PORTIA SAILED THROUGH THE HALLWAYS, sang out loud in the elevator, and dared those creepy shadows to come out when she reached the sixth floor.

The hallway shadows did not engage.

But inside her apartment…

She opened the door to find Jane, quite bright, standing in front of the sofa. The ghost seemed happy, at least for a dead person. Then Portia thought she understood.

"You heard what happened, didn't you?" She bounced into the apartment, a giggle on her lips, without closing or locking the door. Portia was too happy to worry. And why should she? After all—

A searing, mind-wrecking pain exploded in her head before the world went black.

EVEN BEFORE HER EYES OPENED, Portia knew she was bleeding. A lot. Her fingers dug into the carpet's plush pile and found it drenched. Her eyes opened… focused. Jane stood over her, bright and three-dimensional. "Why… why did you do this?"

"She didn't do it, Miss Portia."

If she had been able, Portia might have gasped. But she found any sharp breath or movement brought blood bubbling into her mouth. "Juanita?"

The young woman's troubled face came into view. She was crying. "I'm sorry Miss Portia. But I… I needed my break, too. Miss Jane told me she would hook me up with a rich man if I helped her pass on out of that board. I tried to give it to some of them bitches, but they wouldn't touch it. You… you, Miss Portia, you was the only person I knew who liked creepy stuff so… I'm sorry it was you, but you understand. I don't want to be a maid. I want to live upstairs; you know?"

"Please… Juanita, you're killing me."

"No, no, not like that. You won't be dead-dead, Miss Portia. You're just going to take Miss Jane's place, okay? She'll be able to get out and when the time comes, you'll get out, too."

Portia grabbed the only play she thought she had. "She's a demon, Juanita, and she's lying to you."

Juanita grinned. "No, ma'am. Miss Jane never lied to me. To you, but not to me." She held her left hand where Portia could see it. "That ring has real diamonds. Gave to me by her son, mister, I mean Frank. Frank and I will get married, and Miss Jane will pass on to heaven to start a new life."

"Juanita, please…"

"Don't worry, Miss Portia. I'm going to take the board to a pawnshop. You won't be in there long." She danced out of Portia's failing vision.

"Juanita?"

"She's gone." Jane squatted next to Portia and took her wrist. "Don't worry. Juanita's right about some of that, but I won't be going to heaven. My son's going to pick up my body from the cryogenic storage where it's been for the last few months. I'll return to my body and then send Juanita's little gold-digging ass on her way."

"How…" Portia couldn't form the words. She was so tired.

"There, there." Jane patted her arm. "The board needs company, my dear. Even a demon hates being alone on Thanksgiving."

Darkness closed in from the corners of the room… or maybe her eyes. Portia's lids were so heavy… and Jane was fading…

PORTIA OPENED HER EYES in a darkened room with a strange, ambient glow. She saw nothing around her, and the world tipped and swayed when she tried to sit up. Calls for help couldn't find their way out of her brain.

When the disorientation diminished enough for her to stand, Portia looked for the source of the light. It came from above, sifting through oddly shaped skylights. Memory seeped in with those tiny rays.

She grabbed at her chest, feeling for the knife wound, but it wasn't there. Neither was she wet nor sticky with blood. She kicked aside any thought of dreaming. Portia knew what happened was real. "Hello? Where am I?"

Again, she turned her attention to the skylights, the openings with such strange shapes… "That's an X… Y… A… Oh, God, no!"

The demon's head appeared above her in the dark between the letters, smiling.

DECEMBER

WHAT MAKES AUGUST GROVE such an interesting place is its people. Its population is diverse and growing more so every year. Yet, the old ways hold strong, even as the new world creates a place for itself in our fair town. But change never happens without… complications. Compromises must be made, new lines drawn, and tweaks and adjustments made to the "natural order."

I am the August Grove Herald, and even I feel the effects of change.

But a few things seem immune to it. The universal relationships between men and women; husbands and wives; parents and children—at their core, they never seem to change. The love and honor; the pain and issues… they're always there. Especially as change, fueled by time, pride, and growth, exerts its influence on human dynamics.

Husbands and wives.

Mothers and daughters.

Fathers and sons.

Especially this father and son.

The young man you're about to meet has grown up in his father's rather substantial shadow, a shadow that smothered him.

"A Loser Is, As A Loser Does." That has always been Paul Doggey's motto. And Paul, Fire Chief of the August Grove Fire Department for almost twenty years, passed that pithy slogan on to his son, Mark, who, at 9:45pm on December 24th, Christmas Eve, is hanging off the side of the Crayton County trestle. For Mark, this is…

A DEAD MAN'S CHRISTMAS

MARK DOGGEY HAD A VIEW of August Grove he'd never seen before. From his vantage point, he could see the entire length of the oversized gulley that people called the Crayton Ravine. He was at the outer edge of town, but he could still discern the difference in the lights—their brightness, the candy colors, and even the decorative lighting on the grand steeple of the August Grove First Baptist Church.

Under other circumstances, Mark might have enjoyed the scene. But hanging from a bridge on the year's coldest night didn't give him a lot of room for pleasure.

Hanging.

He wasn't sure what held him there, but it was sharp. The usual suspects—a screw, nail, bolt, even an old railroad spike—all seemed unlikely. Every time Mark tried to wriggle out of his jacket, to finish the fall into the rocky hole below, something stabbed him in the back. *But I have to get loose.*

Get Loose. For a moment, he wondered why being crushed at the bottom of a ravine was a better way to die than to be stabbed and bleed out? *Dead was dead, right?*

"No. I don't want to hang around for hours, bleeding out." Steam bloomed from his mouth with his response. "Or freeze to death, for that matter."

As always, he answered himself out loud. Part of Mark's problem, in his opinion, was spending too much time inside his own head. He was frequently at odds with his inner self, and since he didn't have many people to talk to, his inner dialogue often slipped out. The habit of talking to himself hadn't made him a lot of friends, either.

"What a loser." He shook his head, which produced a sharp stab just below the base of his neck. "And now I can't even die right."

"And exactly, how do you die… *right*?"

The question came from above, Mark thought, somewhere on the bridge. Duh, where else would it come from? *No angels out looking for wings tonight, dumb ass.*

"Yeah, that movie inspires a lot of people to do what you're doing… or I should say, *trying* to do."

Mark was certain that deep, manly voice had a smile in it. Hell, he hated this guy already. He had waited twenty-seven years for his voice to change. He was pretty sure it never had. "What the hell do you want?"

"Me? Shouldn't I be asking you that question? I mean, do you need a hand or a rope or an ambulance seems like a better ask, right?"

"I'd say screw you, jerk, except talking is making whatever's holding me jab me in the back. So, I'm shutting up."

There was a pause, maybe some movement, but then nothing. Mark's adrenaline popped, and he got that trembling rush that only fear can cause. Funny, when he jumped, he hadn't been afraid. He hadn't even been afraid when he got hung up. Pissed, yes, but not scared. Now, his heart raced a little too much to deny his anxiousness. "Hey… Hey! You still there?"

"Yeah, Mark. I'm here."

"You know me?"

There was a quick chuckle. "Dude, there are a million guys like you. You drank the Kool-Aid, swallowed the crap, bought the lie… and all the other phrases that mean you believed the nonsense people told you. Who was it? Your old man?"

"How… how did you know?"

The guy sighed. "Conventional wisdom says there's no user's guide for parents. But yeah, there is. They just don't read it. Or they get the version with half the damn pages missing. Or, more likely, they misread the name of the chapter called *Ten Quick and Easy Steps to Screw Up Your Offspring*. It's funny how many of them miss the title of that section before they dive in."

"But for sure, there's one tip those parents always latch onto, the item that says, in bold text, 'Be an Overbearing Asshole to Your Child.' That 'My way or the highway' shit. They think that's the only way to raise a squared-away kid. Especially a boy. And then they don't understand when their kid either hits the bricks, grows up to be a major prick, or hides within himself and becomes what your old man calls a loser."

For almost five minutes, Mark couldn't speak. Memories crashed through him like waves against a cliff. Sharp and hard, bold and blunt, recollections of the yelling, the beatings, and his mother crying rushed in. And yeah, him attempting to hide in plain sight couldn't be left out. Mark had spent his entire life trying to disappear. "Uh, that was quite a rant."

"Sorry. I receive a lot of calls like this one, especially at Christmas. And tonight, your call came in early, so I decided to come to see, this time, what drives an otherwise decent human being to want to end his life. Not that suicide isn't decent. Sometimes it's even noble. But a lot of times, it's just a person who needs help who can't get it. So, I'm here, Mark, and there just might be a little help on the rails for you."

His visitor laughed at his lame joke, Mark thought. But he also said help… for him. "You can assist me by removing whatever's holding me up here… so I can finish what I started."

"That was lamer than my joke," the man said.

"Hey! Are you reading my mind? How did you—?"

"I'm not here to answer questions. I'm here to get answers. So, explain this crap to me. Why do you believe going splat in the bottom of that hole will end all your worries?"

That adrenaline was back, but this time it fired off an ounce or two of anger. "What kind of question is that? Nobody worries once they're dead. Splat. Kaput. Problems solved."

"Who told you that shit?"

"What do you mean? Dead is dead."

"Dead is most certainly dead." The guy sighed. "But there are at least fifty flavors of dead, and not all of them put you in the ground. For example, how high is this trestle? And why are you so certain the fall is going to kill you? Want to hear a real loser's move? Hit bottom, break every bone, and live. And guess what? The pain isn't in the waiting and the healing. Nope. The pain is in knowing that everyone knows you jumped. You jumped! You tried to kill yourself and failed. Life as you knew it is over because the world isn't ever going to forget that."

"Uh, yeah... I... I know." Mark couldn't wipe the tears spilling from his eyes. The warm moisture slowed as it traced its way down cold cheeks. "I... I checked. Somebody jumped off this bridge before—"

"Trestle. Not a bridge." The man said it with annoyance. "You can't even lie and say you fell off a bridge. This is a trestle, and there shouldn't be anything up here but a damned train."

"Fine, whatever. Some guy jumped off this trestle before and they found his body a couple of days later. And he was stone, cold dead. So there."

"So, there?" The howl of laughter continued until Mark couldn't take it.

"What's so damned funny?" He squirmed. "Ouch!"

"Yeah, it hurts, doesn't it? Well, trust me. Lying in the bottom of that ravine, alternately hoping someone will find and help you, or wishing you had died on impact... Neither is funny. The guy that jumped... yeah, he could tell you how not funny that was. He died less than two hours before the search party thought to check the ravine. I mean, why would they? The man, as far as anyone knew, was in his right mind. Why would he be lying down there, sprawled across a bunch of rocks, dying in one of the worst ways possible?"

"You... you can't know that." The sharp thing dug into his back. Now Mark felt warm blood drizzling over his freezing skin. "Are you going to help me or what?"

"Yes, I think I will. I'm going to show you how that guy died." And with that, a strong, cold palm clamped onto Mark's head.

"Hey, what are you doing?" Mark tried to move, to get away. But the more he squirmed, the deeper the blade—and he was certain now that it was a blade—sliced into his flesh. But it was poison or poison, be cut or get fried, because the guy's hand was getting hot. "Let me go, you creep! What the hell are you doing to me?"

"First, I'm keeping your dumb ass from freezing to death," the man said. "So shut up and quit fidgeting while you're still in one piece. And close your eyes. What I'm about to show you might make you dizzy."

Mark had to admit his cold quakes had stopped, so he tried to relax. But his mind returned to the obvious. This man hadn't changed his situation much. He continued to dangle off the side of a bri… uh, trestle, and whatever held him was slicing him into baloney.

And his new buddy was letting all that happen.

"Can't you pull that thing out of me?" Mark asked.

"If I do, you hit the ground." Matter of fact, no squeamishness or qualms, this guy.

"Who the hell are you?" Mark asked.

"Hell didn't send me. Now, like I said, be still. You need to see this."

"See whaaaaa…" The rest of Mark's words died in a scream.

Night… gone… darkness… vanished.

The ravine, in daylight, rushed toward him… no, him toward the ground. So fast. Yet, he didn't hit when he expected. The fall continued. On… and on… and on…

And then the pain… collision… That should have been reversed, but it… No. He felt the impact in his mind before he hit. Then his body exploded. The force shattered him from the inside out, the concussion so violent his brain wasn't capable of processing it all at once. So, the pain came in devastating waves, swelling against his nerves, and then slamming through his mind. Death by brute force.

Death…

The death he expected didn't come.

"Oh, God…"

Those weren't words, they were sensations—a plea for mercy, redemption, and rescue in a single pulse before it drowned in suffering and terror.

He had punctured a lung… maybe both, filling with blood, and he couldn't breathe. His jaw was broken, and even though Mark thought his mouth hung open, a scream for help was an idea crushed under the heel of his agony.

Somehow in his non-seeing eyes, the world shimmered, and he once again hung from the trestle, a warm dampness in his trousers, and tears on his face. Both evaporated… dried in seconds. The whimper that escaped him flew away, ignored as his mind wanted to do nothing but thank God that he wasn't at the bottom of that ravine. "Oh… oh, God."

"That's a joke I won't do. I don't answer when people call to God." The deep voice settled to almost a whisper. "I'm sorry. But I wanted you to understand that there are no easy ways to go out unless you're at home in your bed, underneath your woman, or sound asleep, dreaming. Hear me? That's the way you want to die. This, what you're trying to do now, is wrong and useless."

"It… useless?" Mark was still experiencing, and enjoying, the slamming of his heart, the stinging ache in his back, and the quaking of his freezing limbs. All that discomfort meant he still resided on planet earth. "Why… why?"

"Why?" The boom reemerged in that baritone. "Because of that garbage you swallowed. You convinced yourself that everybody would be sorry when you were gone and own up to how they wronged you. Right?"

His teeth chattered, but Mark stuttered out, "Ye, ye, ye, yeah."

"Let's take a walk."

Mark gasped as something lifted him higher into the air. For a moment, he hung, weightless as a feather, over the chasm he had been trying to reach. His breath caught in his throat so hard it couldn't fuel the scream his mind wanted to make.

In the next instant, whatever held him swiveled toward the trestle, like the arm of a crane. The pain in his back vanished at the same time his support disappeared, and he dropped to the rough-hewn timbers a few feet below. Mark, his knees trembling, his muscles turned to jelly, collapsed when his feet touched solid wood. He resisted his impulse to kiss the railroad ties, but he laid his face down to the splintery surface and wept.

"Come on, Mark. It's cold out here."

So glad to be alive and in one piece, Mark had forgotten about his strange benefactor. He got to his knees before his eyes sought the...

Man?

Mark's "thank you" disappeared, frightened out of existence. "Holy…!"

"Not quite."

His eyes kept blinking, as if to make the vision before him change, while Mark forced his mouth to close. From his angle, the… man… possibly… seemed seven feet tall. He was, yeah, tall, black, with thick dreadlocks almost to his waist. He wore clothing in midnight shades, from his long leather coat that barely kissed the ground, to the rest of his attire. And in his hand…

Mark's mouth opened and closed several times before he could speak. "What is that?"

The man, his eyes shining, golden, turned to his left and regarded a gigantic blade… at the end of a thick handle… silver and gleaming…

Horrifying.

"That? Oh, that's a scythe." The guy shrugged. "I don't use it much. In fact, I think it's been over a hundred years since the last time I called that thing. It's too big."

And as he said those words, the blade shrank, the long handle diminished, until the scythe was no more. Instead, the man held a silver sword in his hand. A sliver of light raced along the blade as he lifted it, and bloomed at the tip into a tiny star as the weapon vanished.

Mark's body screamed for him to move… crawl… run away. But he couldn't.

The man smiled, bright white teeth gleaming. Mark remembered how the stories about Lucifer always said he was handsome. Maybe this was he—tall, dark, broad like a linebacker, and ridiculously good looking. "You taking me to Hell?"

The giant glowered down at him, his golden eyes sparking. "I don't do the devil's dirty work. I'll repeat, Hell didn't send me."

The guy strode toward him, and it was then that Mark noticed the shiny leather jump boots. Soldier? A large, dark hand reached out to him. "Come on, dude. We've got places to be."

His entire body quivered, but Mark reached up and took the man's hand. It was warm and strong, and the callouses on his palms indicated he once worked hard at something.

"Th… thanks." On his feet, Mark noted the man… if he was a man, was not much taller than he at six-foot. And those golden eyes were now a light brown, but they still seemed to shine, even in the dark. "Uh, so, where are we going?"

"Remember that movie I mentioned? I forget the main character's name, but an angel showed him what life in the town would be like if he'd never been born."

"Yeah, that's right." Funny. Mark loved that movie, but he couldn't remember the main character's name either.

"No matter, because that's not what we're doing," the dark man said. "We're going to see the aftermath of you dying tonight. I want you to see the guilt and sorrow you're needing."

"I don't really—" Mark began.

"*Shadow Rider*!" The man yelled.

A roar. It was a sound unlike anything Mark had ever experienced—deeper than an ocean, darker than the night, and absolutely blood chilling. It penetrated his flesh like some kind of sonic wave. He'd heard lions and other animals at the zoo, roaring and growling. But this…

The timbers beneath his feet trembled, and his bones did the same.

"What… what?"

It appeared as if materializing from darkness. Part of his mind was the little boy back at the Fernbank Museum, eyes wide and amazed at an exhibit of prehistoric animals. The seven-year-old Mark stood eye to eye with a saber-tooth tiger, and he couldn't get the grin off his face.

He wasn't grinning now.

The gigantic beast was at least four feet tall, and its long legs and massive head became visible as if it stepped through a wall of smoke. Its upper canines, long and flat like daggers—and probably as sharp as those blades—gleamed in the dim light.

Mark's feet danced as his thoughts skittered. *Tiger… ginormous… probably hungry… monster… killer beast… real… It's real. It's coming!*

The man strode away to meet the animal.

"That's… that's…" Mark took several steps backward… but stopped, his teeth chattering. Part of him knew to stay still. This was an alpha predator, and if he ran, it would be on him in a second. But the other part of him, possibly the sane part, couldn't stop shaking.

"Mark, this is *Shadow Rider*," the man said. The great cat rubbed its head against the leather coat. Sparks like tiny stars erupted from its black fur when it did. They twinkled about the man and tiger before disappearing.

"That's a…"

"Yeah, a saber-tooth, but he's just a big kitty. Aren't you, boy?" He scrubbed a hand down the cat's broad back, and again, tiny stars flared out into the night. "He's our ride."

The tiger growled and lowered its head as if agreeing.

"Oh, what the hell!" Mark shook from his jittering feet to the tips of his fingers. "I'm crazy. That's it. I'm lying at the bottom of the ravine, mad with pain, my sanity completely gone. This is a damned dream. All of it."

"It will seem like a dream tomorrow." The man hugged the neck of the prehistoric, and very extinct, creature. "But it's not a figment or hallucination tonight."

He stopped speaking and stood for a moment, his head tilted, regarding Mark. "I'm sorry for scaring you. A subtler approach might have done the job better. Let's start over." He extended a hand. "My name is Condor. And this is my spirit beast, *Shadow Rider*."

Mark was taking small steps backward even as the man offered his hand. "What… what the hell are you? Demon? Angel?"

The man shook his head, dreads swaying. "Nope, neither. In the supernatural hierarchy, I'm somewhere between. Higher than demons, but lower than angels." He turned to the ebony feline and tweaked its ear. "We are not divine beings. Death is my, not his, boss." He bounded up onto the tiger's back. "I'm what humans call a Reaper." He grinned. "And there's nothing grim about me."

He returned to the tiger. "Time to go, boy."

The tiger roared.

Mark nearly fainted.

The cat's golden eyes gleamed as it spread its legs and lowered its head. Mark gaped as the broad shoulders narrowed, the fur vanishing, revealing gleaming steel. As he watched, bone and muscle hardened to metal—front legs and paws to forked rods and a wheel…

What happened in the rear, Mark did not see. He couldn't take his eyes from the bulging chest as it morphed into a chromed-out engine and gas tank. From head to tail, the ebony saber-tooth tiger became a low, sleek, black motorcycle. It rumbled as the transformation concluded, but there was a deep growl beneath that sound.

Condor took hold of the handlebars and grinned. "This is my boy! Come, hop on."

Mark desperately sought that inner child, the kid who would be amazed and excited and overjoyed to hop onto the back of a magical beast turned motorcycle. Every one of those words would have sent young Mark careening into the man's arms. He'd probably beg to drive. That's who he was… in the beginning.

But now, after two decades of belittling, degrading, dismissive behavior from those he respected… of being reminded what a loser he was at every turn… that energetic, creative, live wire of a boy was gone. He didn't write or draw anymore. He didn't speak out, talk up, or make himself known anymore. Mark had become invisible, even to the two people he thought loved him, his mother, and Dianne. He suspected Dianne had finally given up. She'd been waiting for him to become a man since high school. Tonight, he'd seen her with another guy at the best restaurant in town. Yeah, she'd waited long enough.

And so had he.

"This won't accomplish anything," Mark said. "I mean, so what if people are sad? What difference does it make if my father regrets how he treated me? I'll be gone."

Condor stared at him, and the gold returned to his eyes. "Exactly. You're getting there. But there's more, and for that, you need an in-person visit."

"Visit?" Mark had to recall his tongue as it scurried into hiding. "Uh, we're riding?"

"Don't worry about Shad." Condor revved the engine, and Mark's hair momentarily stood on end. "He's a pussycat, but just wait until you see my kitty run."

The grin on Condor's face reminded Mark of what absolute joy was. Could he have that, once again, before he called it quits?

"Yeah, why not? If I'm going to take a final ride, why shouldn't it be outrageous?" He trotted to the bike but halted at the side of the machine. It was monstrous. "You're sure he won't mind?"

A gurgle, almost like a purr, emitted from the enormous engine. A gleam skimmed along its chrome, and the black metal trembled.

"That's an invitation if ever I've seen one," Condor said, smiling. "All aboard!"

Mark laughed, nodded, and did indeed climb aboard. He had to stretch his legs to straddle the tiger-turned-machine. But once he settled behind the Reaper, the amount of comfort and excitement he felt surprised him. "Let's ride!"

Condor laughed. "You heard the man, Shad. Carry us where we need to be. And take the scenic route."

The cycle roared, more animal than machine, and the wheels spun, smoked, before it leaped forward. Mark grabbed onto Condor's shoulders, digging his fingers into the soft leather, and howled. The sensation was simultaneously like being on something with four legs, running full out, while also having a rocket under his butt. The wheels left the ground often, and that's when the seven-year-old came out to play. He screamed, laughed, and yelled for Condor to go faster.

The Reaper obliged.

The narrow road leading away from the trestle crossed a bridge over Highway 118. The motorcycle veered right and flew over the bridge's guardrail and into open air. It continued forward, the wheels spinning, finally descending slowly down to the highway.

And all the while, Mark whooped and screamed his heart out, having the most fun he'd ever had in his life. The world blurred around them as the big cat roared down the highway, blowing the doors off cars and setting the asphalt on fire. Condor immediately repaired the damage they wrought, but Mark still imagined the cars as fallen adversaries, lying on their sides, their underbellies exposed to their conqueror, the fastest machine in the world. He couldn't have stop laughing if he'd tried.

THE CLOCK ON THE PORTER-SMITH GRANARY silo at the edge of town ticked along at 11:51pm when the tiger bike's wheels touched down gently on asphalt and it slowed to a prowl. The low rumble of that beast was downright sexy, in Mark's opinion. Though, he had to admit, at the moment, his logic, emotions, and opinions might be a little impaired. He had only been high once in his life... before tonight. This had weed beat all to hell!

He slapped his face with both hands to knock some sense back into his silly brain. Mark wanted to fly through town, straight down Broad Street, fast and loud and laughing like a total loon. That's what he wished, but Condor was no fun. He fell against the Reaper, giggling. That seven-year-old had total control.

But his demeanor sobered the closer they got to his parents'
home. "Do we have to go there?"

"For less than ten minutes," Condor said. "Promise."

As they rode through August Grove, smoke swirled up from
chimneys, and what passed for snow in the southeast lay on a
few of the lawns. It would all be gone an hour or two after
sunrise, except in the shadiest places. Kids would ride their
new bikes or whatever kids did on Christmas Day. The weather
wouldn't be a deterrent to anything. Mark grinned. He might
go to the park and shoot a few hoops. He hadn't been there in
years.

And that's when he realized something was changing. He'd
stopped going to the park because he hated the grief the guys
heaped on him. Nothing serious or malicious. He wasn't a runt
at six feet tall, and he wasn't a terrible player. But his skin was
so raw from his dad's continuous flaying, he took everything
from everyone as a personal attack. Maybe dying had allowed
his outer shell to heal.

Shadow Rider slowed to a crawl on Bertram Drive. Mark
squeezed his legs tight against the bike's hard steel, but felt the
slow, sinuous movement of thick muscles. For a moment, he
thought it might be worth dying to ride such a wondrous
creature.

Condor spoke back over his shoulder. "No, it really isn't."

The saber-tooth motorcycle made no sound as they stopped
in front of the two-story ranch. Mark had grown up in that
house, lived there as he got his degree from the local college,
and moved out to the small loft space over the garage when he
took the job as Administrative Clerk for the August Grove Fire
Department. Clerk. He hated the job. It was just another hook
where he hung around to be a punching bag. And his father was
just fine with letting his men do it.

He leveraged himself off the motorcycle, careful not to let his boot drag across the seat. Mark even found enough courage to pat the wonderful machine. "Thanks for the ride, *Shadow Rider.*"

The creature rumbled softly.

"He likes you," Condor said.

Mark shook his head, feeling the joy and laughter sloshing around inside like his mom's best eggnog. The spiked kind. "If I tell someone… told anyone… they'd never, ever believe…" He spun and waved his arms in the air. "Any of it." But the house pulled his gaze back to life's reality like a magnet. Mark settled his gaze there for a long minute before turning back to Condor. "Uh, are you coming inside, too?"

Condor shook his head. "No, you might want to go this one alone."

"No… I mean, I wouldn't mind company… to explain all this." Mark looked at the house. "I'm not sure I know what to say."

Without Mark's awareness, Condor had somehow detached his long legs from Shadow Rider and now stood beside him. "You won't say anything. You're dead, remember? At least for now. Your folks won't see you. You're here, just like in the movies, to watch. To see who you were in their eyes. OK?"

Mark nodded. "This won't be good, will it?"

"Have a little faith, man. You might be surprised. Now, take my arm, inhale, and…"

When he exhaled the breath, Mark stood in his parents' living room. He and Condor were situated to one side of the Christmas tree, facing the center of the room. He hadn't sensed a thing when they… whatever moving without moving was called. And even if he had, that sensation would have died the instant he saw his mother.

His mom sat on the sofa, crying, and his father was on the phone, pacing back and forth. "Yeah, I'll be down to do all that tomorrow. Okay, thanks." He ended the call. "I'm going down to the coroner in the morning—"

Cheryl Doggey fell sideways onto the cushions and screamed into a pillow.

Mark's heart shattered. He took a step toward her, but Condor grabbed his arm. He shook his head and said, "You're here to observe. No one can see you. No one will hear you. Now, watch."

His father dropped to a knee beside the sofa. "Cherry, it's going to be alright."

His mother continued to cry, sobs shaking her entire body.

Paul Doggey stood, rangy and tall, his face creased in every way possible. "I promise, it'll be all right."

When Cheryl turned her head and looked at him, her tears still ran, and scars from her grief still marred her face, but her eyes… Red surrounded the cool blue orbs and they sizzled with rage.

Paul took a step backward.

"How dare you, Paul! Promise? Promise what? Can you bring our son back? Or should I say my son?"

"Cheryl…"

"He was never your son. You didn't want him and you never missed an opportunity to let him know it." She was sitting now, glaring up at him. She was a foot shorter than her husband, but as she rose from the sofa, she seemed to stare him straight in the eyes. "You drove him to this."

"That's not true," Paul said, his voice shaking.

"Which part?" She took a step toward him, and once again, Paul gave ground.

"What's happening here?" Mark asked. "I've never seen my mother like this."

"Like what?" Condor asked.

"Unafraid." Mark stepped closer to his parents, where he might see his father's face.

Paul straightened. "I tried to be the best father I could to that…"

"That?" Cheryl yelled. "That what? What were you going to say? And you can stop lying now. Mark's gone and he won't be back to embarrass you anymore."

"Cheryl, I did all I could." He reached out to her, but she smacked his hand away. He stiffened. "What the hell did you want? For me to forget? Every time I looked into his face, it reminded me of what you did. Not that he didn't look like me. He had to, didn't he, since my brother was his father?"

Mark's mouth dropped open, and before he could close it…

Cheryl stepped forward and smacked Paul hard enough to make his knees wobble.

With his upper body twisted away from her, Paul pressed his left palm to his reddening cheek. But as he turned back to Cheryl, his right hand slowly balled into a fist.

Mark lunged toward the man he'd always called "dad," but found himself pulled backward. He slid, as if on ice, across the floor to Condor's side.

"My mom… I'm not… My uncle Hank…" Babbling. And Mark couldn't slow his mind enough to regain control of his mouth. "She had an…"

"Shut up and listen," Condor said.

Cheryl gazed down at his fist, but then glowered up into his face. "You don't get to bully me into acting like I did something wrong, Paul. Never again. When you hit me, I'm walking out the door to tell everyone what our life is. Was…

because I'm through, understand?" Tears flowed. "If I hadn't been a coward, I would have left long ago. My son is dead because I didn't."

Paul dropped his hands and stared at her, his face reddened and twisted by rage and pain. "Yeah, remind me again that Mark was *your* son. Only yours."

"And whose fault was that?" Cheryl asked.

The man's hand was a blur as it struck her. It was an open-handed blow, but it spun her in place.

"Oh, he's not doing that!" Mark raced to… and through… Paul. He turned and gaped. "What the hell?"

Paul stopped and looked around, shivering.

That gave Cheryl the time she needed to recover. She grabbed a figurine, a carved wooden swan, from the coffee table. She held it in her fist as she swung upward, into her husband's chin. This time, Paul Doggey went to the floor.

Cheryl stood over him, her hand already swelling from her broken middle finger. "Your fault, you ass. Yours." She seemed finally to notice the pain and let the little swan fall to the floor. She held her injured hand to her chest, but kept her eyes on the swan as she spoke.

"You don't get to make me feel like a whore anymore. I loved you enough to live without children. But you couldn't have people thinking the great Paul Doggey wasn't all man, could you? I slept with your brother because you begged me to. I slept with your brother because you said it would be better than adopting. The child would have your blood." She turned burning eyes on Paul. "*Our* blood. But in the end, coward that you are, you couldn't go through with it."

Paul sat up and snarled at her.

"Oh my God." Mark gasped. "Look at him. He hates her."

"Look again," Condor said. "The person he hates is himself."

"I begged you to have an abortion." Paul got to his feet slowly. "I asked you not to make me think… think about you and Hank together… all those nights."

"Four times. Four. It was hardly a long-running affair."

"It was enough." Paul got to his feet. "Enough that Hank fell in love with you."

Cheryl dropped her swollen fist and stared at him, wild-eyed. "What?"

"Oh, what the fuck?" Mark almost spun in place, alternating his attention between them. "What hell is this?"

"Didn't you wonder why Hank stopped coming around?" Paul walked to the fireplace, wiping blood from the scratch on his face. "He told me he couldn't take coming here, seeing us together. I had you and his son." His voice cracked as the tears flowed. "That baby cost me everything—you and my brother."

He turned slowly, once again facing her. "I could never… I couldn't believe you didn't love him, too. When Hank was here… around you… that's when you looked happy."

"I want to leave now." Mark's words fell from his lips like lead pellets.

"Wait four more minutes." As Condor spoke, the doorbell rang.

"Let it ring," Cheryl said.

"It might be the police." Paul wiped his chin again and headed for the door.

Cheryl never moved. She stared ahead, and Mark's heart stopped beating. His mother… so much grief and agony. All those years.

Paul reentered the living room with a dark-haired young woman at his side. She was roughly the same height as his wife, and she, too, was crying. "Cheryl, this is Dianne. She's a friend… she knew Mark."

Mark took a step forward, but he stopped for a multitude of reasons. "Dianne. What… what is she doing?" He settled for reaching, but not trying to touch her. "Di… why is she here?"

Condor didn't answer.

"I'm so sorry, Mrs. Doggey." Dianne glanced up at Paul as if unsure of what she should say. When her gaze returned to Cheryl, her lips trembled with her words. "So sorry. I… I…" She burst into tears.

After a moment of apparent surprise, Cheryl rushed forward and pulled Dianne into her arms. "Oh, my dear, we didn't know. He hadn't told us."

"Mom, it's not what you think." Even in death, Mark's face heated. "Those are sympathy tears."

"I loved him so much," Dianne said.

Condor grabbed his arm when Mark's knees failed. "Hang in. We're almost done."

"I was on my way here to get him… Mark… to introduce him to my oldest brother. He just… he just got back to town…" she spoke between sobs. "I had hoped… Oh, I can't."

Paul patted her shoulder. "We know."

To Mark's surprise, his father… uncle… had tears in his eyes as well. When his mother looked up at him, he held out his hand to her.

She took it.

The three of them stood in the center of the room and cried together.

The clock on the mantle above the fireplace chimed. Condor clamped onto Mark's arm. "We gotta go."

"But… I need—" He was astride Shadow Rider when the rest of those words came out of his mouth. "—to know what they're going to do."

"You can find out tomorrow," Condor said. "Take us there, boy."

There was no ride that time. Mark grabbed onto the Reaper's shoulders as the big bike rose slowly from the ground… and vanished.

It was the most awful cold he'd ever felt. And even though it lasted only a second, Mark thought he would never be warm again.

When light returned, he was once again hanging off the Crayton County trestle.

"Decision time, son." Condor's booming voice hurt Mark's ears.

"What decision?"

"Are you going or coming? Jumping or staying?"

"I have a choice?" Mark tried to remain still, to ease the pain from the scythe. "I get to choose?"

"You're human, so yeah." Condor's words rang like chimes within him. "You have free will, Mark. There are always options, and you can always choose. The question is, will you make the right choice? What's it going to be? Life? Or death?"

"I… I'd like to live. Please."

That laugh Mark thought he hated rang out. "That's what I'm talking about!"

The world went dark.

Mark thought Condor might have left him in that freezer an extra second as punishment for being stupid. When he opened his eyes, he staggered on the trestle. And then he staggered again. "Uh, why do I feel drunk?"

"Were you drinking before you came out here?" Condor hugged *Shadow Rider's* neck as the big cat nuzzled him. "Shad says yes."

"How… how does he know?" His words tilted from his mouth a tad east of true north. "Who told you, Shad?"

Condor laughed. "He can smell it. 'Hooch,' he says."

Mark tottered sideways as he laughed. He corrected his movement and stopped, but he had to hold on to the ground to stay put. He looked up at Condor from his squat. "Uh, guess I am. Too drunk to drive."

The Reaper chuckled. "Yeah, I'd say so."

Shadow Rider roared, and Mark fell back on his rump. He gawked as the big cat vanished.

"You've got a nice walk ahead of you," Condor said.

"What?" Mark struggled to his feet. "You… you're not taking me back?"

"I didn't bring you out here, so nope. Not." Condor laughed. "You're back where you were, with perhaps a little more sense in your head. You won't remember what happened tonight, but you will feel it. So will your folks. And things, for all of you, including Dianne, will change." He strode forward and grabbed Mark's hand to shake it.

Mark, instead, lunged into Condor's arms. "I… I don't know how to thank you." He buried his face in the lapels of the leather coat. "They… they made hard decisions…"

"To have you. They both wanted a child to love, to share." Condor pushed him back. "But ego, anger, and poor communication make for a hot mess. Listen. None of you are too young or too old to fix this, OK? You can make this right."

As Mark listed to the right, Condor took hold of his shoulders. The Reaper, his orbs a golden blaze, stared into his eyes. "Remember this: You have to bring them together on Christmas day and make them talk to you. Make them!" He tapped Mark on the forehead. "Remember that."

Mark reeled while blinking away tiny stars as his head filled with rushing wind and… roaring butterflies? He straightened and stared around. He was alone.

"Hey! Not even halfway?"

He heard, from a distance, that boisterous baritone guffaw. Mark smiled, tugged his jacket closed, and staggered off the trestle toward home. With each step, the cold sobered him. And with each mile, the evening seemed more like a dream.

In the full light of morning, he woke in his bed, still dressed, thinking he really needed to have a talk with his folks.

DECEMBER 31ˢᵀ

THE OLD YEAR EASES AWAY as easily as tired memories, sometimes taking pain with it, but other times opening old wounds. In its passing, the old year might even create a few new scars. Tonight, both things will happen for one of my favorite people.

Detective Gerald Betters is not in August Grove on this New Year's Eve. He is at his home in Atlanta, but the tug on his heart and mind from our town is strong. Still, he resists, because Gerald, more than many, believes it's his duty, his life's purpose, to do the right thing. Even when others will not. He's risked his life, more than once, when living by that mandate. Thus, he's home in Atlanta to fix things. He's home to make things right, even though he's the one who has been wronged. He believes, if he squares things for everyone, all that he desires will be his.

Unfortunately, as the clock's hands move closer to midnight, he learns his first mission has failed. The woman he thought he loved as married another man. The work assignment he wanted has been given to someone else. And now, as he packs a bag to travel to a friend's wedding, he learns the new year will begin with him being a three-time loser.

So Much for the Holidays

GERALD BETTERS eyed his cell with a certain amount of trepidation. He didn't think he could take another hit of bad news tonight. All he wanted to do was get his stuff together and get the hell out of town. He'd start the new year in another place with different people and hopefully, a better frame of mind.

The phone rang again.

He didn't recognize the number, but he answered anyway. He was a cop. Cops don't ignore their phones. "This is Betters."

"Hey."

"Hey yourself. I'm finally packing. I think my plane lands in Chicago at three tomorrow. You're meeting me at O'Hare, right?"

"No. I'm not in Chicago."

"What? Where the heck are you?"

His friend laughed. "No need for you to fly. I'm in Atlanta. At the airport waiting for my next flight to board."

"Seriously? What's going on? You and Lainie decide to elope?"

He was quiet, and Gerald's left arm began to itch. "What happened?"

"I need to talk to my friend, Gerry. Not Detective Betters."

The itch worsened. "What the hell's happening, Tom? Where's Lainie?"

"Gerry… If you're Gerry, pull up a chair and listen. I've got 30 minutes before my plane takes off, and I've got a lot to say. So, are you listening?"

Gerald dropped onto the end of the bed. "Yeah. Yeah, I'm listening."

"Good, because I'm going to tell you a story. I'll get it out before the year is over, and we can both start the new one with no baggage."

Gerald glanced at the clock. 11:28pm. He'd never get to the airport in time. Before he could respond, his friend started talking.

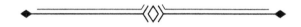

I STOOD IN THE ALLEY and stared up at the biggest man I'd ever shared air with.

"OK, let's talk price."

McShane loomed over me, seven-and-a-half feet tall if he was an inch. His fetid breath blew out of his face like exhaust from a fouled engine; a face wide and ugly with a pug nose that must have been broken at birth. His eyes, round, black, and flat as the bottom of cast-iron skillets, glared at me.

The alley was blind—one way in, one way out. Only one door on any of the buildings, and he planted his gigantic frame between me and it, his massive paws resting on the wall to either side of me. He sniffed once, and then stood up straight. His hat disappeared into the dark above the alley.

I wiped away the sweat beading under my nose.

"You get what you pay for," McShane said. "You paid cheap for the old man, and you got a sloppy job. Led me right to your doorstep. But you'll pay me good because I don't work cheap, and the job will be tight because I'm a professional."

GERALD SAT UP on the bed. "Wait, Tom. Stop. Are you telling me that you met with a hitman? Were you undercover? What the—

"Shut up, Gerry. It's 11:40. We don't have much time."

THE GUY PREENED and stuck out his big chest like he was king of the world or some shit. I tried to look up into his face, but the top of my head only reached midway his chest. All eight-feet of him and six-feet wide so the only detail I could make out was a chipped button on the shirt straining across his gut. "How… how do I know you're what you say you are?"

"So, it's proof you'll be wantin' then." He laughed. "My portfolio, that's the word, ain't it? Well, I've got one for you. Remember banker man out in Windwood last year? Coppers still got nothin' on that one. That's 'cause I'm clean. Took him with his wife sleep right beside him. In and out, broke his neck, less than twenty minutes."

He spat what smelled like tobacco juice at my feet. "And just so's you know, my kind of professional ain't cheap."

"No. I mean, I understand." I tried to get a view out of the alleyway, but he was too broad. Probably ten-feet wide. I stepped to the right, up against a garbage can reeking of yesterday's cabbage. "I'll… I'll need more… examples, because this, this is a special job."

"What's so special about it?" He stared down at me, his eye beams beating me on the top of the head from at least ten feet up. He growled. "This izza revenge killing, ain't it?"

I straightened my back, tried to be taller. "Yeah, I want the bastard dead."

"What bastard? What did he do?"

"Killed my fiancé," I said. "Killed her as she slept in the bath. A waitress, and she'd been working hard all day. She just wanted to relax. Killed her before she could even get out of the tub. So, you'll need to tell me you can do something… similar."

He rocked his humongous head back and roared. "You came to the right man. There was some killings—a massacre, the newspapers called it. One city block – e'rey man, woman, and child, even cats and dogs—all dead. Killed in a single night." He stuck out his chest again, pushing me tighter to the wall. "All by me, savvy? All by meself."

"Why?"

McShane shrugged. "'Twas a wager. Ones like me, we take pride in what we do. Killin' is art and science. We in the trade is always competing to see who's best. I took on a challenge, proved I'm the greatest of 'em all. One city block, thirty-eight souls, all in one night without nary a scream. Clean. No weapons and no trace of me left behind. Cops haul me in now, I ain't worried. They'd have nothin'. No proof. No evidence."

He pounded on his chest with a gigantic mallet of a fist. The sound echoed down into his gut, beating on my eardrums… hailstones the size of baseballs. "Me fellows still rave about it."

I swallowed hard. "A wager? How much?"

"Twern't the money. It was the pride, the fame. A dollar's all the wager was; a dollar to seal the deal."

"A competition…" The words rang in the alley with a thunderous echo. "You killed… all of them… on a bet?" The words slid across my tongue like razor blades.

He grinned, bearing yellowed teeth and whatever he'd had for dinner. "Aye. One evening. Just a handful of hours."

I slid farther to the right, shoving the garbage can as I moved into its place. Then I pushed it forward, just beyond the big assassin, giving me a view of the end of the alley. "So, you did all the people by yourself."

"Yeah. Funny thing, too. I did a girl in a bathtub that night." His grin broadened.

"I know." I removed my white fedora and held it up into the light of the bulb hanging from the back of the restaurant that had dumped its rotting cabbage in the can.

"Whatcha mean, you know?" McShane bent to stare into my eyes. Not nearly as tall as I thought. In fact, not much taller than myself. His left eye fluttered and his right eye twitched. "What you doin'?"

"That was my fiancé in the bathtub, and I'm killing the bastard who murdered her."

The bullet made no sound as it penetrated his thick skull, but I imagined the noise the hollow point slug made, disintegrating into a million shards inside his arrogant head, shredding his little brain to kibble. I imagined the bits of metal singing as they went about their work, taking pride in laying waste to that flesh.

Professional.

The murderer dropped soundlessly to the ground, all six feet of him, his gut escaping the dingy shirt imprisoning it. I stood over him and watched every millisecond of his life as it ebbed away. I gazed down into those eyes as they died, and I hoped he could see my face until the end.

The man behind the rifle soon joined me in the alley. Quiet. Professional.

McShane's eyes stared blindly into the night sky as his killer reached across the dead body and took his payment from my hand. "What old man was he talking about?"

"Dunnoh," I said. "He got some bad information somewhere."

The guy smiled before dropping a dollar bill onto McShane's corpse. I didn't ask what that was about, but I suspected it had something to do with a wager. He nodded and strode away into the night.

I considered the man at my feet, calculating the number of lives he'd taken, the weight of the misery he'd created. For years, he had ended lives with impunity, destroying families and devastating friends. I didn't think anyone would be sorry he was gone. I pulled my phone from my pocket.

"This is Lieutenant Tom Wilson. I need backup..."

Gerald's thoughts vacated his mind like sand pouring from the bulb of an hourglass. The clock on the bedroom wall was supposed to be silent, yet its steady tick boomed into his ears, into his skull like thunder. Like that bullet.

He was empty. Weak... or the phone somehow altered its composition. The weight of it caused his arm to drop, his hand to flop, release the phone to the mattress. The surrounding space blurred into a confusing array of shapes and frizzing color...

"It... it can't be." Gerald hung his head.

Tick... tick... tick...

A voice... far away... calling his name...

Somewhere, that infamous Betters obstinance whispered, "But. It. Is."

As the world came back into focus, the detective realized the thunderous noise in his ears was the sound of his heart shattering. Tears welled in his eyes… the itch in his arm stopped… his heart thudded… He raised the phone back to his ear.

"What… what the hell are you telling me, Tom? Is Lainie… Lainie's dead? And you…"

"I'm starting over, Gerry, like you should. We both lost the loves of our lives, just in different ways. We both lost the jobs we love. Just… differently."

Gerald thought his life might be falling to pieces with sound effects. Something like glass shattered somewhere… not in the here and now, but sometime.

"Tom, listen—"

"No, you listen, Gerry. Life is short, and there's more to living than that detective's badge you value so much. You were learning that before everything fell apart." Tom sighed. "A new year is upon us, as they say. A new beginning. Don't try to pick up those old pieces of your life. They're bent, twisted, and broken. Start over. Walk away. Embrace the new year with a fresh start. Trust me, you'll be glad you did. And Gerry?"

Gerald exhaled harshly and raked a hand through his hair. "Yeah?"

"Don't come after me."

The call ended.

Detective Gerald Betters lay back on the bed with his phone on his chest and contemplated the ticking of the clock. One minute until midnight.

Tick… tick… tick…

Thirty seconds until the end of the world.

Tick…

The old pieces of your life are bent and broken.

Tick…

"Embrace the new year with a fresh start."

Tick.

Gerald raised the phone, pressed a single button, and waited. After three rings, a woman's voice came on the line. Cops don't ignore their phones.

There was music and the sound of a party in the background. "Happy New Year," she said.

"I hope so," Gerald said. "Do you still need me for that job in August Grove?"

So, we come to the end of your visit. I hope you enjoyed your time in August Grove. There are always interesting people and interesting times in our fair city. Come again.

Because I am
  the August Grove Herald.
    I always have stories to
      tell.

And never fear, Sybil always knows how to find me. Just visit her website at sybilward.com.

See you soon!

THANKS!

Thank you for reading *Holidays in August Grove*.
For more stories and inside information about upcoming
August Grove adventures, get a **free** copy of
The Story Storm
Newsletter.

SCAN THE CODE BELOW

https://sybilward.com/freecopy

Coming in January 2024

Get a sneak peak now. Turn the page for Chapter 1.

August Grove Collection

presents

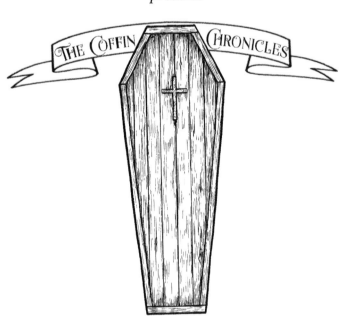

HOLE CARDS

AN AUGUST GROVE ADVENTURE

SYBIL WARD

PLEASE ALLOW ME to make a few observations.

People who live in sprawling urban areas, or just well-populated cities, seem to think everyone in a small town knows everyone else. That might be true in the tiniest, most isolated areas. But you can, in most places, on any given day, pass someone on the street, in a school, or at a grocery store that you have never seen before. A complete stranger.

And of late, we are less open to strangers. Especially since that nasty little bug raced around the planet and killed so many of us. We are, despite seeking "friends and followers" on the Internet, less open to people when outside our front door. In real life.

And there's always something, or some… thing… to make you glad you're not so all-embracing.

But those "things" often come calling at home. And sometimes we even recognize the faces they wear. But when those things are unknown, or even worse, unseen… Well, that's when genuine terror happens. That's when everyone becomes a stranger. A suspect. An enemy. Something to fear.

And fear doesn't care about the size of your town.

At the moment, fear is alive and thriving in August Grove, Georgia. It's bold, feeding and growing on tortured hearts, and stretching its way into a full-grown terror. Fear is feasting, thanks to the twisted evil descending on the town.

It's an evil without a face.

An evil without a name.

No one has seen it. Nobody knows it. Just the grief it leaves behind.

A friend once told me she wished she knew everything. I smiled as I told her to be careful what she wished for. Knowing everything isn't a gift. It's a curse wrapped up in pretty paper, and the package inside often contains pain, loneliness, and mind-numbing horrors.

I know, because I know everything.

I am the August Grove Herald. And unlike the town's rag of a newspaper, I am a true herald, and I've been one for hundreds of years. It is my blessing, my curse, and my purpose to relay what is occurring and what is yet to arrive. But I can never interfere.

As a Herald, I am compelled to tell someone what I know. That is my purpose. But I can never, ever tell those to whom my knowledge would benefit the most. To do so would bring destruction upon me, and to all whom I have confided.

Thus, is my life. That is my curse.

But you… I will tell you everything. It is you who will bear witness.

I AM THE HERALD.
HEAR ME.

Somewhere on earth, every day of the year, every moment of the day, Good is confronting Evil. As they say, twenty-four/seven. In August Grove, a town in the southeastern United States, one of those confrontations is beginning.

And it begins with Dash Coffin.

THE COFFIN CHRONICLES

*If you must enter a darkened
hallway, make sure you're not
the one walking in front, or
ensure the person behind
isn't carrying a sharp-edged
grudge.*

*Clearly, I never follow my own
advice.*

Dash Coffin

CHAPTER 1

SOMETHING LIKE A TINGLE, then more a twinge, centered itself between Dash Coffin's shoulder blades. She squirmed, the sensation deepening to a hot, not-quite-agonizing slice. As the pain worsened, she considered what Nietzsche meant when he said, "If looks could kill." Glaring pricks. Hate-filled gazes. Staring daggers into someone's skin…

That kind of stuff.

The stabbing pain in her back, directly over the spine, intensified.

Perhaps mirroring her unease, all fifty-three cards of the fifty-four card poker deck she carried in her pocket riffled slightly. Dash patted the jeans pocket, but the gesture did little to reassure her or her cardboard companions. The atmosphere in the musty hallway felt too much like a stroll to an execution.

Dash shrugged and rotated her shoulders as she trudged along, and all the while, her mother's titanium-sharp gaze continued to slice into her flesh. That brand of animosity was not unanticipated. Her glowering and suspicious parent was preparing for her youngest child's next lie. But there wouldn't be one. Not today. Her mother was doing Dash a favor by letting her move back home. Lying to the person doing you a kindness was bad juju.

Even if the provider laced that kindness with venom.

As a child, Dash questioned how her mother seemed able to inflict pain upon her without a single touch. After leaving August Grove, she convinced herself it had been her childish imagination. But the pain had always felt so real. She wondered if her mother's hatred of her had become an actual weapon. Was that even possible?

Shivers barged their way into her already aching back. The ability to weaponize an emotion into a physical threat was a terrifying idea.

At the doorway to her childhood room, Dash's stomach pinched. The place was even smaller than she remembered. With its raw wooden floor, unpainted planked walls, and single exposed bulb hanging from a cord in the ceiling, Dash could think of only one word to describe it. Unfinished. And like her, an afterthought. She took a deep breath and sought the shinier side of the coin. That poor wizard boy had slept beneath the stairs. As a child, that lovely bit of fiction always reminded her there were worse places to sleep than a butler's pantry. At least she'd had a window.

Dash once again patted her pocket, trying to calm the squirming deck within. When the cards were this nervous, it was never a good sign. But they had a lot of nerve getting antsy now. That damned near sentient set of cardboard hustlers and heifers was the reason she was in this current mess. Completely their fault. Must go home, they said. Must hurry, they said. Return now, they said. They had nagged her night and day until she relented.

Not something she wanted to do at all, but she came. She had packed her duffle and got on a plane, another thing she wasn't all that crazy about. The cards had only ever pressed her so hard about one thing, and she hadn't listened. And she'd paid dearly for that mistake. With them raising such a ruckus, she knew whatever was happening was serious. Dash sighed. It damned well better be. She could be somewhere enjoying something. Anything. Anywhere. Except back here in August Grove.

She sighed again. "Home, sweet home."

The words, though hollow in her mind, sounded less like a lie than Dash expected. Maybe because, somewhere beyond the brazen bull of not giving a damn, she didn't lie. She wished it was home. It just wasn't. The cramped and decrepit room held too many ghosts. They collected in the corners like frightened dust bunnies, crumpled boxes of them—church programs and religious pamphlets and "good girl" indoctrination paraphernalia—all reminders of the person her mother had wanted Dash to be.

And the innumerable times Dash failed her.

Louise continued to stand in the hallway, bent over like an owl, eyeing Dash as she always had, as if her child were a zoo specimen or lab rat. The woman would never come into the room; at least not when Dash was in it. She would come and prowl around, search Dash's things, and sometimes trash a book when her daughter was at school. She'd use house cleaning as her reason for being in there, except she never so much as swept an inch. Maybe she'd done so when Dash was a baby, but from the time Dash could remember, her mother never cleaned her room or otherwise stepped foot in it to care for her. Never. She spent all her affections on her sons.

"Just like you left it. Ten years ago." Her mother leaned on her crutch and frowned into the space. "Still your room… Dashira."

Dashira was her given name, of course, but only a handful of people ever called her that. And no one ever said it with the same intonation, uttered it with the same inflection, as her mother. She said "Dashira" as if the very word left a foul taste in her mouth. Louise Williams spoke her only daughter's name like it was a curse.

Suddenly, for Dash, ten years away didn't seem nearly long enough.

A cold, hard lump formed in the back of her throat as she tried to ignore the old feelings her own name conjured for her. Bad feelings, and that was so terribly wrong. No one should ever make a child hate their own name. Dash fought back her mounting rage. Anger, and the cold need to lash out, served no purpose in the here and now. She'd done enough of that in her nightmares. No, she needed to be in the moment. This moment. Instead of giving in to the scream collecting in her throat, she nodded, summoned a rebellious smile, and surveyed her old accommodation.

So much stuff in such a small space. Dash marveled at the amount of junk she accumulated as a child. More surprising was how much of it remained in the eight-by-ten-foot space. She had never attributed sentimentality to Louise—

Funny. Now that she was back home, groveling for a roof over her head, calling her mother by her first name didn't sit right in her mind's mouth. She tried it out. Louise… Mother… Neither felt right, but she knew instinct would fill in the blank when the time came.

Again, the books, plaques, and awards drew her eye. She'd never considered her mother to be a sentimental woman. In fact, sentimentality was a disease her entire family seemed immune to. Except her. Dash had to learn, the hard way, that letting your heart rule your actions could get you killed. She shook her head. Now was not the time to relive that memory.

But oblivious to her desires, as usual, her heart went there. "Is Pete still around the house?"

"Who?" Her mother straightened. "Who's Pete?"

"You know… that one-eared dog that used to hang around." Dash smiled at the memory. "I used to sneak my food from my plate so I could feed him at night. He was a nice dog."

Louise frowned. "That mangy thing is probably dead. I had Animal Control pick it up as soon as you left." She snorted. "Might have called the next day. At any rate, ten years gone. Thing would be dead now, anyway."

"Yeah." Dash sniffed, hard, and turned her back to her mother. That dog had lived under the house, beneath her little room, and they would fall asleep at night—her on the floor with her blanket, staring down through the cracks between the floorboards at his shiny eyes. He always seemed so happy to have company. As was she. Dash hadn't been a little kid back then, maybe ten or eleven, but Pete was still the doll, teddy bear, and old stuffed animal she never had, all rolled up into a warm, living thing. Back then, if she could have found a way to do it, she would have dragged him, fleas and all, up into her bed.

Dash sniffled again. The day she ran, she couldn't… she didn't get the chance to say goodbye to Pete. If only she had taken him with her—

A hard sneeze dragged Dash's attention back to the present.

"That's the dust." Louise rapped the door frame with her metal crutch causing chunky bits of gray to drift to the floor. "I don't get around so well anymore. The entire place needs a good cleaning."

She had told Dash, even before allowing her to enter the house, how arthritis had plagued her for all the years Dash had been gone. In recent months, she'd said with lowered eyes, the disease threatened to immobilize her as it ruthlessly attacked her lower spine.

Dash had recognized the guilt shot and the follow-on play for sympathy. As she scanned the room, she acknowledged her mother might have a legitimate excuse not to clean. Now. But as her tear-filled eyes danced across the dresser, chest-of-drawers, and bookshelf—each covered with a ten-year-old layer of dust, that was as close to sympathy as Dash could manage. Something less than charitable within her concluded Karma was a bitch.

Her mother seemed poised for some kind of response, so Dash said, "Not a problem… Mama. I've slept in worse."

As usual, not the best answer.

"You won't sleep in worse here. In case you missed it, that was a hint to clean your room." Louise smiled, sort of, her tobacco-stained teeth barely showing. "Well, might not be a hint."

Dash nodded and suppressed another sneeze. "You were never subtle." She dropped onto the twin bed and launched a swarm of dusty devils. "And neither is this bed." She leapt to her feet as the powdery shower returned to its resting place.

"Everything for cleaning is right where it should be," her mother said as she limped away. "If you can remember where that is."

"Ouch." Dash thought she'd need Kevlar to make it through the rest of the week. Those shots would keep on coming. Perhaps being here wasn't the best—

Before she could complete the thought, the front door of the three-bedroom house slammed open so hard, Dash felt it in her feet. She didn't have to ask, nor wait for this visitor to be announced. She raced out into the hall, searching for the one person she loved without question.

"When did you get home?" Ardis snatched the bright red bandana from Dash's head, allowing a mass of tight black and red curls to escape. "And damn, your hair."

"Watch your mouth, Ardis," Louise called from somewhere in the house.

"Yes, ma'am." Ardis rolled her eyes before grinning broadly.

Dash squealed. "Look at you, in a dress." Ardis twirled, showing off the dark green coat dress with a black belt at the waist. The patent leather belt matched her shoes. "You look like a friggin' woman in that getup."

"I am a woman. I got to be one while your ass was gone."

"Ardis!" Louise rapped her crutch against the wall. "And you too, Dashira."

"Yes, ma'am," they chorused. The cousins grinned as Dash grabbed Ardis's hand and dragged her into the tiny bedroom. She closed the door and waited, her ear to the only painted surface in the room. Within a minute, the soft thump of Louise's crutch made its way to her door. Dash put a finger to her lips and shushed Ardis, who shook with laughter.

"I wore a dress like that to the Conway Baptist Church Revival," Dash said, her voice ringing in the small space. "I swear, I saw the light that day."

The harrumph from the other side was loud enough that Ardis heard it across the room. Grinning, she slapped a hand over her mouth as Dash whispered, "Some things never change."

Louise, either satisfied or disappointed with her eavesdropping, nonetheless retreated. The thump of her crutch ebbed as she exited the hallway.

Dash waited half a second after the final thud before she squealed, rushed to Ardis, and flung her arms around the taller woman's neck. "I've missed you so much."

Ardis returned her hug and raised it to a giant squeeze. "You, too."

Her cousin was a year older than Dash, but they had always been together. Some people called them the midnight twins. Dash never understood the midnight part, unless it was a reference to their coloring. She and Ardis were both dark-skinned, much darker than their mothers and siblings. Probably inherited their coloring from their fathers—whoever they were. Aunt Mandy, aka Miranda Walsh, married the light-skinned Tyson Walsh right out of high school and had two sons in three years. Like Dash, Ardis hadn't come along until much later, and she didn't resemble her mother or the man she called daddy.

Infidelity ran in the damned family, was Dash's thought on the subject. And thank God. Ardis was the only person in the entire bunch Dash could tolerate. In her opinion, because they were "outside children," they had missed out on the Asshole gene.

"Tell me everything," Ardis said.

Dash grinned. "Help me clean."

"Yeah, nothing changes." Ardis laughed and headed to the door. "Talk. I'll get the vacuum." She vanished into the dark hallway.

Dash eased the deck of playing cards from her jeans pocket and let it lie flat on her left palm. For an instant, the edges glowed a deep golden-yellow, and an electric thrill raced up her arm. She flipped the Archangel deck in her hand to view the face of the bottom card. The Joker smiled up at her, the epitome of innocence, its eyes glowing. Dash squeezed the deck gently. "Don't grin at me. As much as I love Ardy, you'd better have a damned good reason for dragging me back here."

End of Excerpt
The Coffin Chronicles :: Book 1
HOLE Cards

A MESSAGE FROM SIR JONASHIR OTTHERIN KANDASIRE, EARL of RUSTERRIM
aka MY LADY'S JOKER

So, dear reader, what do you think? Did the cards and I bring Dash Coffin home for a good reason? And what do you think of Dash? My lady has many issues, not the least of which is a contingent of crooks out for her blood. But she is a woman of courage and conviction, and we of her magical deck are always at her side, to aid and protect her. But sometimes, we are not enough.

Can Dash find the babies, help the police apprehend the kidnapper, and get out of August Grove with her lovely skin intact? Or is her mother's flaying just the beginning?

Read more for free. Subscribe to the *Story Storm Newsletter*, and get the first five chapters of *HOLE Cards*. Pick up where you left off, and see what trouble we've gotten Dash into.

https://sybilward.com/subscribe

MEDIA AND OTHER CREDITS

Graphic assets for the creation of covers and interior images were created with Midjourney AI, stock images from Pixelbay, iStockphoto, and Dreamtime.

Fonts from Google Fonts (fonts.google.com), Myfonts, 123RF. com

Interior formatting via Affinity Publisher.

Image creation with Corel's PaintShop Pro

A REQUEST, PLEASE

Wherever you bought *Holidays*, please leave a review. If you'd like, please review and talk about it on social media. Your words leave a lasting impression and will really help me get the word out about my books.

And let me know if you're talking about it. I always send huge virtual hugs!

About the Author

NOTHING SPECIAL ABOUT ME. I might be old… possibly… but only as much as the world allows. In my opinion, I'm too old to have an age, having been born with most of my opinions intact, believing my own theories long before embracing those of anyone else. Ancient is probably a better word for my state of mind. And from that, you may well guess, my stories are also born full-grown.

But am I stuck in my ways, resistant to change? Never! The Geek Flag flies high and proud around here, with a total embrace of technology, new ideas, and great comic book movies. Change without hate, scorn, or the demeaning of anyone at anytime, anywhere. Embracing the future means accepting what's best about NOW.

In this life, I've been a daughter, a student, a seamstress, a soldier, and a wife. I fired an M16, taught basic electronics, repaired communications encryption equipment, and potty-trained wee ones—not necessarily in that order—and spent a fair chunk of my life in MOM school. I'm a web designer, a crafter of scrapbooks, and maker of journals.

And between eclipses, a writer.

Where I live, there is silence, noise, construction, and destruction. And it all makes for an interesting life.

That's it. I hope you found something in the ramble that makes you want to stay and be friends. We can share a cup of Coke, coffee, or even tea. I'll let you choose.

Printed in Great Britain
by Amazon